Prescott is bored, lonely, and even a little jealous. While he feels bad about that last one, he can't do anything about it. Everyone in his flock have found their mates, and they're so lovey-dovey Prescott wants to gag. It wouldn't be so bad if he could go out and search for his own mate. Unfortunately, due to the unrest in the shifter community and his flock living with a councilman, the estate is on lock-down. Tired of it, Prescott sneaks out and heads to a new dance club. He intends to dance and get laid, but what he discovers is so much more.

When Nkosi Akintola follows Prescott into the men's room, they realize they're mates. As much as Nkosi wishes he could bond with Prescott that instant, he can't. He's a black mamba shifter on an undercover mission, and timing is critical. As a member of the rogue shifters trying to topple the Shifter Council, Nkosi knows his duty must come first, even before his mate. After giving Prescott the information Nkosi has gathered, he takes the wood duck shifter home.

When Nkosi returns from his mission an injured man, will Prescott forgive and accept him?

Undercover Snake
Copyright © 2020 Charlie Richards
ISBN: 978-1-4874-3028-3
Cover art by Angela Waters

Published by eXtasy Books Inc or
Devine Destinies, an imprint of eXtasy Books Inc

Look for us online at:
www.eXtasybooks.com or www.devinedestinies.com

UNDERCOVER SNAKE
SHIFTER'S REGIME BOOK FIVE

BY

CHARLIE RICHARDS

DEDICATION

The measure of intelligence is the ability to change.
~Albert Einstein

CHAPTER ONE

"Oh, gods. Faster. Harder."

Upon hearing Lachlan's throaty urgings, Prescott froze just inside the door.

"Gods, yessss," Thad rumbled huskily. "So good."

Prescott felt his face heat as blood rushed south. For a few seconds, he paused to listen to his flock-mates fucking. He was also damn tempted to round the tables and chairs to find them so he could watch.

I bet they're sprawled out before the fireplace. I could watch Thad pound away at Lachlan's toned form.

Except, Prescott didn't. Hearing flesh slapping against flesh, he backed away. The sounds of grunts and groans mixed with whispered words told Prescott that his friends were barreling down the homestretch.

Exiting the library, Prescott closed the door quietly. His own cock ached behind the fly of his jeans, and he rubbed at himself. He toyed with the idea of tracking down Bashir. The vampire was always happy to enjoy a quick fuck and blood donation.

Thinking of the sensations created by Bashir drinking his blood, Prescott moaned. His dick twitched, and a bead of pre-cum oozed from him. Even his balls began to tingle.

Then Prescott remembered Bashir was off the property on some assignment for Seever.

Lucky bastard.

With the troubles caused by a bunch of rogue shifters targeting the shifter council and those associated with it—led by a bigoted ex-councilman with a penchant for shifter trafficking—the estate where Prescott and the rest of his flock lived was on lock-down. They'd moved there a couple of years before when fellow flock-mate Cho had met his mate in Shifter Councilman Vincentius Goldstein. For everyone's safety, they couldn't leave the estate without quite a bit of protection.

Prescott wondered if some other guard would be up for a quickie and started down the hall in search of someone to scratch his itch.

While Prescott knew many whispered about him being the estate slut, he didn't care. After all, it was true. Prescott had loved sex as soon as he'd discovered how pleasurable it could be. Having spent decades locked in a cage, mostly trapped in his wood duck form, he enjoyed as much touch as he could get.

Pushing memories of his time being experimented on by scientists from his mind, Prescott searched out a partner for some horizontal fun.

Three days later, Prescott bit back a groan as he stood frozen in the doorway to the kitchen. He'd wanted a mid-afternoon snack. Instead, he'd stumbled upon Reese, the human who worked as the estate's chef, enjoying an afternoon delight with his lion shifter mate, Seever.

The grunting coming from the massive pantry could be nothing else.

Prescott growled as he pivoted and stalked out of the kitchen, his hunger gone. In fact, he didn't even end up aroused by the sounds. A different kind of warmth churned in his gut.

Jealousy.

Rubbing at his chest, Prescott felt a wave of guilt flood him. He shook his head, but he couldn't seem to help himself. While he figured his flock-mates were using sex to decompress from the stress as well as pass the time, Prescott didn't have a mate.

And I want one.

Man or woman, old or young, fat or thin—Prescott didn't give a shit. He didn't care what his mate would look like. He just wanted to find him or her. Unfortunately, with still being on lock-down, Prescott couldn't go out to look.

Sighing, Prescott headed to the entertainment room. He spotted his alpha, Ashton, cuddled up on a sofa with his mate, Ranger. While the scent of sex lingered in the air, they were fully clothed.

Glad I missed that.

Prescott would never want to spy on Alpha Ashton with his mate. His alpha would scratch his eyes out of his skull.

"Hey, Prescott," Ashton greeted him with a relaxed smile.

Yeah, I know what put that look on his face.

"Hi, Ashton," Prescott replied. "Ranger."

"Prescott." The black-backed jackal shifter snuggled against Ashton, a well-fucked flush still darkening his tanned cheeks. "We're gonna watch a movie. Join us?"

Prescott crossed to the bar as he replied, "Yeah. Sounds good. What were you thinking of watching?" It didn't really matter. He was that bored.

"We were talking about doing a *Lethal Weapon* marathon," Ashton told him. "The rest of the guys should be here in ten."

Snorting while pouring a glass of red wine, Prescott shook his head. "It might be a few more minutes than that if Reese and Seever are supposed to be joining us."

"Oh?" Ashton cocked his head. "Why do you say that?"

With a wink, Prescott crossed to a window and opened it. Then he headed to a second one, so there would be a cross-breeze. "They weren't done, like you guys are." Soon, the light draft began to clear away the scents of sweat, arousal, and semen from the room.

Both men grinned broadly, completely unrepentant.

As they should be.

Ashton cupped Ranger's jaw and held his mate's gaze. "Can't help myself." With a tug, he pulled the other man closer and sealed his lips over the jackal's.

Biting back a sigh, Prescott went about prepping the first movie.

"Oh, shit. I found one," Prescott whispered in shock. "A hole."

Damn.

Prescott's discovery was both a blessing and a curse. On the one hand, the right thing to do was to immediately bring the oversight to Seever, so he could fix the problem. After all, having a hole in security was dangerous. On the other hand, Prescott now had a way to sneak out.

And that new club opened two weeks ago.

When Prescott had begun searching for gaps in the rotation of the guards a couple of weeks before, it had been something to alleviate his boredom. He couldn't sit for hours and read like Thad or get lost in his computer like Cho. Even Hector and Rocky were kept busy with Rocky's toddler, Jayden. The others had jobs, duties to perform.

Prescott didn't really have anything, although he dusted and kept his own rooms cleaned. That didn't take up much time. At this point, he was practically climbing the walls.

Unable to resist the allure of the opportunity, Prescott made his plans. He put together a club outfit and tucked it into a small backpack. After adding his make-up and shoes, he donned black sweatpants and a black tank top.

Leaving his satchel on the bed, Prescott headed to the entertainment center. He would have to wait until Rogan went on shift in two hours. Plus, he needed to figure out everyone's plans for the evening.

Fortunately, clubbing was a late-night activity, so Prescott had plenty of time.

That didn't ease his nerves . . . or his excitement.

"Hey, you okay, Pres?" Gilbert asked, his gaze lowering to Prescott's leg before returning to his face.

Prescott stilled his bouncing leg and thought swiftly.

"What's wrong?" Gilbert's black brows furrowed, and he leaned forward, pulling a little away from his Kodiak bear shifter, Hess. "We'll help if we can."

Clearing his throat, Prescott decided on a plausible response. "Um, I know we can't go out and do much right now, but there's this new movie I really want to see," he began slowly, working out everything in his head. "It's a sequel, and I really want to be able to see it in the theater. Can we arrange a day trip?"

"What movie?" Ashton asked curiously.

"The new *Jumanji* movie," Prescott claimed, seeing he had everyone's attention. *Great.* "I really liked the reboot with Dwayne Johnson, and I want to see the sequel in the theater."

Stop talking. You're repeating yourself.

"I wouldn't mind seein' that myself," Hess revealed, scratching at his goatee. "We could do a matinee."

Ashton exchanged a glance with Gilbert, who acted as their flock's beta. Gilbert explained, "A matinee means it's a movie before five in the evening on a weekday. A lot of theaters offer a discounted price then."

"I'll talk to Vinnie tonight about timing and bodyguards," Cho piped up, lifting his focus from his laptop. "He's in a meeting right now."

Cho was the only one able to get away with calling Vincentius by the pet name. The councilman would ream anyone else who tried it. Naturally, as mates, he wanted Cho happy, so he didn't correct him.

"Thanks!" Prescott grinned. He really did want to see the movie, so it made a great cover.

To Prescott's relief, everyone returned their focus to other things.

At just before nine, the pairs began to filter out of the room—Cho had left over an hour before after getting a text from his mate. There was a bunch of kissing and some light petting going on. They said their goodnights amidst purrs of pleasure and giggles of delight.

Prescott waved at Ashton and Ranger, the last couple in the room. As soon as Prescott no longer heard their footsteps, he rose and hurried to his own room. He strained his ears, so he could avoid everyone.

Once Prescott reached his bedroom, he grabbed his small duffel, shoved his feet into a pair of sneakers, and headed back through the house. To his relief, he managed to escape the mansion without being spotted by anyone. He hid behind a stone patio wall, waiting for the guard patrol to pass.

Fortunately, the guards were more focused on searching the perimeter as opposed to looking toward the house. At one point, Prescott had entertained the idea of shifting to his wood duck form and flying out of the estate. He'd nixed it, since his small form didn't have the strength to carry a satchel full of clothes and shoes.

Spotting the opening Prescott wanted, he made his way to the side gate. He watched as one of the patrol guards paused and talked to Rogan at the gate. A second later, Rogan grabbed the back of the man's neck and pulled him into a deep lick-lock.

While Prescott hoped he didn't get the guards in trouble, he took the opening and crept out of the estate.

As a shifter, Prescott had great stamina and speed, and it didn't take him too long to jog into town. He found a discreet location and changed into his club clothes. With his duffel slung over his shoulder, he entered a gas station and used their bathroom to style his hair and put on his make-up.

Grinning, Prescott left his duffel hidden in the station's air vent, then proceeded to the club.

Even before Prescott turned the corner, he could feel the thumping vibration of the club's music vibrating the ground beneath his feet. He picked up his pace, anticipation filling his veins. It had been months since he'd had the opportunity to dance and enjoy the thrill of rubbing his body against so many others.

While Prescott could get laid on the estate, he loved the opportunity to explore someone new.

Plus, my mate isn't on the estate.

Prescott didn't entertain much hope of finding his mate at a dance club, but he knew it could happen. After all, Hector had met Rocky at a club. Rocky had been the bouncer there, and it had taken several weeks for the bouncy shifter to convince the reserved human he was serious.

Dismissing thoughts of his flock—and pushing away the guilt of sneaking out—Prescott opened the door to the club. His senses were immediately assailed by the scents of alcohol, testosterone, and arousal. The thumping of the music pounded in his ears.

"Well, hello there, cutie," the bouncer greeted. He sat on a stool near the door of the small foyer area, obviously there to check IDs if necessary. "You're a breath of fresh air."

Grinning at the broad-shouldered human, Prescott gave the big man a thorough once-over. "Glad you think so," he replied, licking his lips. "You're not so bad yourself."

The man moved closer, lifting his big hands. "I think I'm gonna have to frisk you." He waggled his brows as he continued, "This club has a no outside food or drink, and a no drug policy, you see."

"Of course." Prescott lifted his arms up, bent at the elbow, and placed them behind his neck. "Always a good policy to have."

"Glad you understand," the bouncer replied.

Then he began running his hands over Prescott—*all* over

him. He even went so far as to blatantly feel up his groin, causing Prescott's dick to harden.

"Mmm, forward." Prescott bucked his hips into the man's fondling grip. "I like."

"I haven't taken my break yet this evening," the man purred into his ear. His words were barely loud enough to be heard over the music coming from the next room. "I could call someone to watch the door if you wanna get a drink with me."

Turning, Prescott peered up at the man. Being six-foot along with the extra two inches from his black dress boots, he only had an inch or so to look up. He rested his hands on the man's shoulders and rubbed over the hard, cloth-covered muscles.

"Only if the drink comes with a sword and two olives," Prescott stated, rocking his hips and blatantly grinding against the man. As a shifter with a high libido, he could easily get off two or three times an evening if he found willing partners. Considering the way the human had felt him up, Prescott figured he would be willing to be partner number one of the evening.

Yeah, I'm a total slut. Oh well.

Obviously catching his meaning, the bouncer squeezed his ass and nodded. "Give me two minutes to get a replacement," he ordered as he dug his fingertips into the crease of Prescott's ass.

"Hurry."

The bouncer stepped back, pulling his phone from his pocket. While glancing Prescott's way, he shot off a text. Then he winked and moved back toward the stool.

"I'm Baden, by the way," he claimed. "You new in town?"

Prescott shook his head. "A couple of years now, but it's been a while since I've found time to get out." He tapped his chest. "Prescott."

Baden grinned broadly, showing off even white teeth. "Well, I'm pleased you decided to grace our club tonight."

"Me, too."

Just as Prescott said the words, another man joined them in the front room. He glanced between Baden and Prescott and smirked. "You know, you're supposed to let them get in the club first, B," he stated, using the back of his hand to smack Baden's upper arm.

Baden laughed and returned to Prescott's side. "Can you blame me, H?" He wrapped his arm around his waist.

"Not one damn bit." The man, H, winked. "Enjoy your break."

"We plan to," Prescott claimed with a laugh, letting H know that he wasn't offended by his insinuations. After all, they were right.

Prescott pressed close to Baden's side as he guided him through the club. The smells whirling around him caused blood to flow south. He'd always loved the aromas of arousal and masculine sweat.

The sight of the people dancing on the floor to the left drew a hum of anticipation from him. He couldn't wait to get amidst all those writhing bodies. His inner duck preened at the idea of being stroked and rubbed by them.

Soon.

Baden led the way directly into the men's room.

Prescott didn't mind. He was hard as a rock, and he wanted the chance to rub all over the broader man's muscles.

Once they were inside, Prescott glanced around the space. He noticed feet in the handicapped stall, so figured they would need to wait. Reaching toward Baden, he thought of a way to pass the time. Prescott enjoyed the feel of the human's arms around him as well as the large bulge pressing against his own.

Rubbing against the human, Prescott leaned in, intending to kiss Baden.

"Well, Prescott, this is not what I expected."

Turning his head upon hearing his name, Prescott stared at

the slender, black man standing just inside the door. He stood maybe five-foot-nine with a wiry frame. His black eyes glittered as he stared at him.

Prescott opened his mouth, intending to ask, "Do I know you?" Then the stranger's scent hit his senses.

Shifter. Mate.

"Oh, fuck."

Chapter Two

Well, *fuck a duck.*

Nkosi Akintola nearly smirked as the expression popped into his head. It seemed that, per Fate, he would be doing that very thing very soon. While he'd never met the shifter standing in the human's arms, he knew he shared his spirit with a wood duck.

Too bad it's really bad fucking timing.

"Do you know him, Prescott?" the human asked, his dark brows furrowing.

Right. My mate is still being held by another man.

Thinking quickly, Nkosi tried to decide the best way to extricate Prescott from the other man's arms without bruising his mate's pride or embarrassing him. His soon-to-be lover beat him to the punch.

"Um, yeah, Baden. He's an ex," Prescott told the human dressed in a polo shirt with the club's logo on it. "We, uh, broke up, and so, um . . ." He seemed to run out of steam.

The human, Baden, nodded slowly, eyeing Nkosi. Then he returned his focus to Prescott and grinned. "Lookin' for a rebound fuck, Pres?" He waggled his eyebrows as he smirked. "You know I'm happy to fill that slot."

Prescott's cheeks darkened, his embarrassment clear. He even appeared to be trying to step backward, but Baden had tightened his grip.

Baden frowned at Nkosi. "So what are you doin' here, man?" He rubbed his left hand up Prescott's side. "Regrettin' what ya lost?"

Nkosi debated the merits of breaking the human's wrist. His black mamba hissed in the back of his mind. His snake would rather bite him and poison him.

Taking a deep breath, Nkosi clenched his hands. "I'm—"

The stall at the end of the bathroom opened, and two men stumbled out. Spotting them, they paused, but only for an instant. The bigger man wrapped his arm around the smaller and grinned, shrugging unabashedly. The smaller man giggled.

Once they'd left, Nkosi turned back to Prescott. "Pres, I'm sorry I told you I wouldn't come out, yet. It was a mistake." Seeing Prescott's brows shoot up, he hoped the wood duck shifter caught on swiftly enough. "The last two weeks without you have been hell. I'll tell my parents, my friends, my coworkers. No more hiding." Stepping closer, Nkosi took Prescott's hand. "You're worth it, my love. You're worth *anything*."

While Nkosi knew his smile was a little hard, he couldn't help it. The asshole human still hadn't released his mate. He tipped his chin toward the guy.

"Even if I hadn't gotten here in time to stop you from fucking behemoth here, I'd still want you back." Nkosi needed to get Baden to remove his hands. "Please?"

Prescott nibbled his lower lip as he nodded. Then he turned to Baden. "I'm sorry. I don't mean to be a cock-tease, but—"

Baden chuckled softly as he released Prescott. "Aww, no worries, man." He winked before grinning widely, his expression relaxed. "After a pronouncement like that, how could you say no?" Gripping the door handle, Baden paused and turned back to them, pointing at Nkosi. "If your man doesn't follow through, you come back and find me, Pres. I'll kick his ass for you."

Prescott's blue eyes were twinkling as he barked a laugh. "Thanks, Baden."

"That won't be necessary," Nkosi stated as he slotted up beside Prescott and wrapped his arm around his waist.

With a shrug, Baden left the room.

Nkosi lifted his free hand and cradled Prescott's jaw. Tipping his head forward, he used his hold to pull his mate's head down. He couldn't wait an instant more to taste the shifter who smelled so divine.

Prescott didn't disappoint him.

The second their lips touched, Nkosi's mate opened to him. He swept his tongue into the other shifter's mouth, tasting and mapping. His duck's flavor exploded across his tongue — sweet and masculine.

While Nkosi was the smaller of them, he pressed Prescott against the bathroom wall and dominated the kiss. He sucked on his tongue and nipped at his lips. Using his hand in Prescott's hair, he guided his chin to the side, allowing him to deepen the kiss.

Nkosi didn't stop tasting Prescott until breathing became urgent.

As soon as their lips parted, Prescott gasped, "Who are you?"

Right. Who am I?

Shit.

Sighing, Nkosi took in Prescott's lust-blown blue eyes, his kiss-swollen lips, and the beautiful flush on his tanned cheeks. His hair was disheveled from his fingers, and he peered at him with a heavy-lidded gaze.

Every fiber of Nkosi's being urged him to drag Prescott into the far stall, to fuck him senseless, and to bite him, bonding them forever.

But he couldn't.

"I'm Nkosi Akintola," Nkosi told his mate. "And this is bad fucking timing."

Prescott's eyes widened. "Nkosi?" He stiffened in Nkosi's hold. "The spy?"

"So you've heard of me?"

Prescott nodded.

Nkosi eased his hold, rubbing his palms over Prescott's chest. He enjoyed the feel of his shifter's toned torso even as he shook his head. Sighing, he attempted to step back.

Growling, Prescott tightened his grip on Nkosi's back. "Where the hell do you think you're going?" he snapped. "I don't care about that shit. You're my mate."

Stilling, Nkosi murmured, "Yes, I am your mate." Sliding his hands up, he massaged Prescott's shoulders, hoping to soothe as he said his next words. "But we can't bond right now, Pres."

"Why the hell not?" Prescott frowned, hurt filling his eyes. "Are you rejecting me?"

"No. Absolutely not," Nkosi instantly denied. He rubbed his thumbs up and down Prescott's neck. "We just have to wait until I'm done with this assignment."

Prescott cocked his head as he swallowed hard enough that his Adam's apple bobbed. "I-I know it would be hard, being separated while you finish, but—" He paused, nibbling his lip, and Nkosi waited patiently. Prescott's voice came out soft and strained. "All my flock-mates have their mates, and I want to know what it'll be like with mine."

Nkosi's snake hissed in his mind. He wished he could agree. He wished he could give his mate what he wanted.

"Bonding would change my scent, Prescott. The rogues would smell it," Nkosi explained. "I saw you at the gas station and thought I'd take the opportunity to pass on some information." Then he frowned as uneasiness hit him. "What the hell are you doing out here without protection, anyway?"

Sighing, Prescott dipped his head, pressing his face against Nkosi's neck. "I was feeling cooped up."

Nkosi instinctively tipped his head to the side, giving Prescott more room. The hairs on his neck stood on end as his mate continued to whisper his admissions. His gut clenched with need, and his cock ached behind the fly of his jeans.

"Lonely. Bored." Prescott lipped kisses along his neck. "Jealous of my flock-mates."

Scenting a healthy dose of embarrassment wafting from Prescott, Nkosi slid his arms around his mate's waist. He rubbed at his back and sides, mapping his ribcage through his thin club-shirt.

"And now I've met you, and I can't have you," Prescott murmured, his voice rough. "Gods." Lifting his head, he gave him a wobbly smile. "I understand. I really do. It just . . . sucks."

Nkosi agreed. It did suck. He wanted his mate just as much as the next shifter.

"I—" Nkosi paused, his mind reeling at the turn of events. Then he realized how and where he was meeting his mate—a human club. Narrowing his gaze on Prescott, Nkosi offered him a hungry smile. "You got a condom and lube?"

Prescott's nostrils flared as he nibbled his bottom lip. He nodded. "Sorry." His cheeks pinked. "I-I hadn't met you, yet. Ya know?"

"I know. That's not why I asked," Nkosi assured, sweeping his gaze over Prescott's muscular frame. "I can't bond us, yet"—he pinned his mate with a feral smile—"but I can still fuck you."

Moaning, Prescott's body bucked against Nkosi's. "Yessss," he hissed as a shudder went through him. "Pleasssse."

"Hell, yeah," Nkosi muttered, his dick jerking. He couldn't remember the last time he'd felt so primed, which made sense, considering this was his mate. "Come on."

Nkosi pulled from Prescott's hold and grabbed his wrist. Leading him into the far stall, he tugged his mate in behind him. With a quick push and pull, Nkosi had the door closed and locked, and his new and forever lover pinned against it, face-first.

To Nkosi's pleasure, Prescott moaned and trembled. The aroma of his arousal increased. He thrust out his ass, obviously just as in need as Nkosi.

Gods, my mate likes being manhandled. Damn, he's perfect.

"Get out the lube," Nkosi whispered into Prescott's ear.

At the same time, Nkosi reached around Prescott and popped each button on his mate's button-fly. The flaps separated, and his new lover's erection flopped into his hand. Nkosi grabbed it in a firm grip and began jacking.

"N-Nkosi," Prescott whined.

"Yes?" Nkosi rumbled into Prescott's ear, having to stand on his toes to do it. The move also allowed him to rub his aching dick against his mate's ass.

Prescott huffed a breath, then waved something in his left hand. "Please, Nkosi. Please fuck me."

"Anything for my mate," Nkosi told him, releasing his erection in favor of taking the condom packet and single-serving lube pouch. "Push your jeans down your legs and spread your legs as much as you can."

With their height difference, Nkosi was going to need him lower.

To Nkosi's surprise, Prescott bent over and unzipped one boot. As he unbuttoned his own fly, his mate kicked off his shoe, then shoved off that pants' leg. The other ended up bunched around the top of his other boot.

Watching Prescott spread his legs wide, lowering himself to Nkosi's level, he groaned roughly. He gripped the base of his dick in a tight hold as he rolled the rubber over his shaft. His head swam as need caused all his blood to flow south.

"Damn, baby," Nkosi mumbled. "Just . . . damn."

With his shoulder pressed against the locked door, Prescott turned his head to peer at him. He reached behind himself and gripped his ass cheeks. His blue eyes held a wealth of pleading.

Then Nkosi saw it . . . the butt plug. His mate had planned to be fucked. He'd been prepared.

A low growl erupted from Nkosi as irrational jealousy surged through his veins. He glared at the offending object. When he returned his focus to Prescott, he saw the blush on his cheeks.

"I-I didn't know you." Prescott whispered the reminder.

Nkosi nodded as he took a deep breath. "Sorry, baby." He tore open the lube with his teeth as he held Prescott's gaze. As Nkosi slathered his erection with the slick, he did his best to reassure his lover. "I understand, Prescott. I really do." While jacking his dick with one hand, he grabbed the base of the plug with the other. Pulling the toy free, Nkosi warned, "No one but me from now on. Got it?" He realized he was being a dick, since he wasn't certain how long he would be under-cover, but he couldn't help himself. "You're mine now."

Prescott nodded, much to Nkosi's relief. "Yours."

Setting the plug on top of the toilet paper dispenser, Nkosi rested his clean hand on Prescott's hip. He eased his slick-cov-ered fingers into his mate's hole—first one, then a second. Curving them, he reveled in the sound of his mate's pleasure, the man's moan music to Nkosi's ears.

"Please, please, please," Prescott chanted, rocking his hips into each of Nkosi's finger-thrusts. "Now, Nkosi. I'm ready. Now."

Nkosi rubbed his left hand under Prescott's shirt, soothing him as he slipped a third finger into the man. Seeing how he easily took it, he pulled them out. He gave them both what they wanted, gripped the base of his shaft, and guided it to Prescott's hole.

Then Nkosi pushed, and at the same time, Prescott rocked back.

Matching groans filled the bathroom as their bodies joined

for the first time. Nkosi watched his long erection disappear inside Prescott's tanned, stretched hole. Heat and suction wrapped around his cock.

Gods, wish I was bare.

Nkosi banished the thought in favor of fucking Prescott. Gripping his mate's hips with both hands, he began pounding in and out of his lover's body. He bucked his hips, grunting his pleasure.

"Gods, Pres," Nkosi ground out through clenched teeth. "Your body was made for my dick."

"Yes," Prescott cried. "Oh, gods! Right there."

Gritting his teeth, Nkosi fought against his urge to come. His balls tightened, and his cock throbbed. His rhythm faltered, and he knew he was seconds away from blowing his load.

"Grip the top of the door," Nkosi ordered as he wrapped his left arm around Prescott's waist. His mate obeyed, and he used his other hand to grab Prescott's cock. "Come for me, Prescott," Nkosi ordered, stripping his mate's twitching dick. "Let me feel how much you like your mate boning you, drilling your needy hole."

Prescott moaned. A shudder worked through his body. In the next instant, he obeyed. His dick pulsed in Nkosi's hand, and his mate's fluids soaked his fingers and the door before him.

The rippling squeeze on Nkosi's erection yanked him over the edge. Holding Prescott tight to his chest, he sank in as deeply as possible. His balls unloaded, filling the condom with spurt after spurt of his cream.

Nkosi's teeth ached, but he managed to keep his mouth shut. His snake hissed angrily in the back of his mind. He mentally hushed the creature even as he enjoyed the bliss of release.

Soon. Soon.

With one more annoyed hiss, Nkosi's snake settled.

"Wow," Prescott mumbled before a snicker escaped him. "Um, we're probably gonna be banned."

Chuckling, Nkosi rubbed his nose along the back of Prescott's shoulder. His mouth watered, and he couldn't resist licking up a bit of his mate's sweat. When he swallowed, he tasted iron and realized he'd bitten his cheek to keep from biting his lover.

"It would well be worth it," Nkosi muttered as he loosened his grip.

Holding the base of the condom, Nkosi eased out while pressing a kiss to Prescott's neck. He grabbed a bunch of toilet paper, wrapped it around the rubber, and disposed of the condom in the toilet. Then he grabbed another handful and helped Prescott clean himself.

After Nkosi straightened his clothes, he helped Prescott get back into his own. He bent and righted his mate's boot so that he could slide his foot back into it. Nkosi zipped it and straightened. Finally, he took the butt plug, wrapped it in fresh toilet paper, and slipped it into the pocket of Prescott's jeans.

Prescott smiled at him, his expression sated. "Thanks."

Nkosi nodded. Touching Prescott's cheek, he told him, "And thank you for understanding, my mate."

Even as Prescott nodded, his Adam's apple bobbed. Dipping his head, his mate pressed their lips together. When he began to press harder, searching for more, Nkosi regretfully pulled away.

Seeing Prescott's hurt look, Nkosi grimaced. "I'm sorry, baby. I bit my cheek pretty deep. Still bleeding."

Prescott's expression turned to understanding. "So, um." He nibbled his bottom lip for a second, a move Nkosi was coming to realize was a sign of nerves.

"What is it, baby?" Nkosi encouraged.

"So, what do we do now?"

Nkosi sighed.
Now, indeed?

CHAPTER THREE

Uncertainty filled Prescott when he spotted the furrowing of Nkosi's brows. The shifter's dark skin crinkled at the corners of his eyes, and his lips pinched. His hands clenched and relaxed where he rested them at Prescott's hips.

"Now." Nkosi drew the word out as he reached past Prescott and unlocked the door. "I drive you home and give you the information I had intended to when I followed you in here."

Prescott didn't fight Nkosi as he guided him to the sinks, so they could wash their hands.

"Then?" Prescott couldn't help but press. He barely refrained from asking, "When can I see you again?" He'd already shown how needy he was by begging for sex.

As they dried their hands on paper towels, Nkosi held Prescott's gaze. "Then our people capture the bad guys, so I can come home, and we can build a life together."

Nkosi threw the paper towels in the trash, and Prescott did the same.

His mate took his hand and squeezed. "We'll get through this, Prescott."

Knowing he had no other choice, he forced a smile and nodded.

Sliding an arm around Prescott, Nkosi grabbed the door handle and opened it.

When Prescott exited, he was surprised to see Baden leaning against the opposite wall. He had his phone out and appeared to be reading. At the sound of the door, he lifted his head and smiled.

"Hey, guys. Glad you're done." Baden grinned rakishly, his brown eyes twinkling. "My break's almost over. Then I'd have to stop monitoring the women's restroom, so I could send guys in to use it between ladies instead of interrupting you all."

Prescott cocked his head. "You were keeping people out for us?"

Baden nodded as he pushed off the wall. "Yep."

"Why?" Nkosi asked.

Waggling his brows, Baden laughed. "Well, you're just getting back together after a two-week separation." He placed his phone back in the holder on his belt as he began walking beside them down the hall. "I knew you'd need a little alone time."

"Wow." Prescott eyed Baden in a new light. "That was awful nice of you."

Resting his right hand over his chest, Baden quipped, "Yep. Heart of gold, right here."

Prescott laughed, and Nkosi chuckled softly.

Baden sobered even as a smile continued to toy around the edges of his lips. "Just because I don't want a relationship doesn't mean I'm not a hopeless romantic." When Baden seemed to notice them both continuing to walk with him toward the front, he asked, "You're not sticking around to dance?"

Prescott shook his head, smiling as he glanced Nkosi's way. "Still have a few things to work out."

"Ah, gotcha."

The trio entered the front to see H checking the ID of a blond. "Okay, man." He handed it back. "Have a good night." Then he looked up at them, only to meet Baden's gaze and arch one brow in question.

Baden shrugged. "Thanks for the break, Hank. I appreciate

it."

H—Hank—nodded, then grinned broadly. "Ended up bein' a ménage, huh?" He barked a laugh. "How do you do it, B?"

Laughing, Baden shook his head. "Naw. Not this time." He pointed his thumb between them. "Misunderstanding between my new friends, and they got back together."

"Well, that explains why I still smell sex in the air." Hank inhaled deeply as he cupped himself, showing off an impressive boner. "Always love that smell."

Baden hummed, eyeing Hank's groin appreciatively. "I hear ya, man." He winked. "Too bad I just had my break."

Hank laughed as he headed toward the doorway. "Not my type, and you know it, man."

Laughing, Baden settled back on his stool.

Nkosi guided Prescott out the door. Taking in a deep breath, Prescott enjoyed the warm evening air that smelled of rain. As soon as the door closed, the music became muffled, although he still felt it beneath his feet.

"Come on, my mate," Nkosi stated, urging him to the left. "My bike is this way."

"Bike?"

Nodding, Nkosi told him, "I'm on a motorcycle."

Prescott eyed the vehicle as it came into view. "That's not like Hess's *Harley*."

The low-slung motorcycle was black, and with the way the seats and handlebars were positioned, it looked like the driver would need to lie over the gas tank.

Chuckling, Nkosi shook his head. "No. This is an *R1*. Very different style of motorcycle."

"Okay."

Prescott didn't know what else to say. He didn't understand, but he didn't drive, either. Gilbert had tried to teach him a few times, but the experiences hadn't been . . . good.

Nkosi smiled, his expression indulgent. "You have no idea what I'm talking about. Do you?"

Shrugging, Prescott admitted, "I don't drive, so it's kinda lost on me."

"If you ever want to learn, I'll try to explain it sometime." Then Nkosi's smile faded as he glanced around the area. "But now isn't the time. Come on."

Unlocking a helmet from a hook, Nkosi held it out to him. "When the time comes, we'll buy you your own helmet. I hope it fits okay."

Prescott took it and put it on his head. "What about you?"

"I'll be fine for now," Nkosi claimed, climbing onto the bike and righting it. "Let's get you home. I have time-sensitive information for Vincentius."

Looking at the tiny seat behind Nkosi, Prescott swallowed hard. "Um." Nerves fired through his veins.

Nkosi held out one hand. "Trust me, my mate."

After taking a deep breath, Prescott took Nkosi's hand and climbed up behind him. He ended up sprawling over his mate's back. With his arms around his lover's waist, he clung tightly as the other shifter started them moving.

Prescott told him where he'd left his clothes, and they hit the gas station first. Fortunately, it was still open.

"No," Nkosi countered thirty minutes later as they approached the estate. "I am *not* taking you to the side gate to sneak back in."

Prescott had explained how he'd left the place, and Nkosi's scent had soured.

"I don't want to get Rogan and Sage in trouble," Prescott explained. "It'll be fine."

"If they are allowing themselves to become distracted while on duty, they deserve to get in trouble." Nkosi glanced over his shoulder at him for a moment—a frown etched across his dark features. "I'm dropping you at the front gate, and I won't leave until you're inside." When Prescott began to protest, Nkosi told him, "They need to fix that problem, for the safety of everyone."

Sighing, Prescott asked, "What if someone sees you? Isn't the estate under surveillance?"

"It is during the day, but no one's on duty right now."

While Prescott understood where Nkosi was coming from, he still felt bad. If he hadn't met his mate, he also would have wished he'd never slipped out. Prescott couldn't feel guilty for that, no matter what happened to the distracted guards.

"Okay," Prescott called over the roar of the bullet bike. That was what Nkosi had called it. He claimed it had to do with the machine's speeding capabilities. Considering there were speed limits on roads for safety reasons, Prescott didn't understand why a machine such as this had even been made.

Just another thing I don't get about driving.

Prescott knew Lachlan was damn proud of his vehicle, too. Even the estate's human mechanic, Pete, thought the Scottish wildcat shifter's car was amazing. He'd even been cheered up after being attacked by being allowed to drive the car.

Wonder what he'd think about Nkosi's bike.

Due to Nkosi pulling up in front of Goldstein's estate, Prescott pushed those thoughts aside. His new lover stopped the motorcycle at the foot of the drive. After helping Prescott climb down, he swung off, too.

"My mouth healed on our drive," Nkosi told him as he removed the helmet. "Give me a kiss for the road."

More than happy to do that, Prescott wrapped his arms around Nkosi. He dipped his head and sealed his lips to his lover's. Sweeping his tongue in deep, he reveled in again being able to taste and explore his mate.

They broke the kiss after who knew how long to the sound of a throat clearing . . . loudly.

Prescott swallowed as he realized Hess stood on the other

side of the gate. His huge arms were crossed, and he leaned against the metal bars. He stared at them with narrowed eyes, and a scowl tightened his lips.

"Prescott," Hess rumbled gruffly. His focus slid to the slender black man in his arms. "You're Nkosi. Aren't you?"

"I am," Nkosi confirmed while reaching over and removing the bungee cord holding Prescott's bag to the back of the bike.

Hess turned his attention back to Prescott. "Get your ass in here, Pres. You're in so much fucking trouble."

Sighing, Prescott nodded. "Yes, Beta-mate," he mumbled before pecking one more kiss to Nkosi's lips and taking his bag. "I hope to see you soon."

"You will," Nkosi vowed. He dug into his pocket and held up a flash drive. "Paraben nearly lost his shit when Sasha was recaptured, and he's growing impatient . . . and irrational." After placing the drive in Prescott's hand, Nkosi squeezed it, then took a step back. "It won't be long now."

With those parting words, Nkosi placed his helmet on his head and turned away.

"Thank you for bringing Prescott back safely," Hess commented from the gate. At some point in the last minute, he'd opened the man-sized door to the left of it.

Nkosi flipped his visor up and eyed the bear shifter. "Anything for my mate." Without waiting for a response, he brought his motorcycle roaring to life and sped away.

Prescott sighed deeply and wrapped his arms around his torso, clutching the bag to his chest.

A second later, Hess's big arm settled over his shoulders.

"Did Nkosi really just call you his mate?" the bear shifter asked gruffly.

Nodding, Prescott left it at that.

Hess hummed softly as he used his hold to turn Prescott and guide him through the gate and onto the estate grounds.

After pushing him onto the passenger seat of a side-by-side utility cart, he rounded it and climbed behind the wheel. Then Hess began driving them to the mansion.

"Why did you sneak out of the estate tonight?" Hess asked after several moments of silence.

Prescott almost just shrugged one shoulder, but he knew he needed to be honest. "Is everyone up?"

"They are."

Grimacing, Prescott murmured, "Can I tell everyone at once?"

"Sure." Hess reached over and patted Prescott's thigh. "Congrats."

Even though his heart hurt from having to watch Nkosi drive away, Prescott still found himself smiling.

I found my mate!

"Thanks," Prescott replied, shaking his head in wonder. "How'd you recognize him?"

"I met him in passing once the day we first arrived," Hess told him. "It's when he gave Cho that first flash drive listing who were sympathetic to Paraben's ideals."

Prescott nodded. "We had to figure out viable ways to get them all out of sensitive positions."

"Right," Hess confirmed. "It took a while, but we did it. Then Nkosi could really get to work helping us bring that organization down."

"Huh."

My mate is kinda a badass.

Prescott smiled for real that time.

By the time they reached the front door, it stood open and nearly every member of Prescott's flock, as well as Vincentius, Seever, and Reese stood under the portico. The only one he didn't see was Jayden, which made sense. The toddler would be in bed at nearly three in the morning.

"In the rec room," Alpha Ashton ordered, a growl in his voice. "Now."

"I'll get drinks started," Reese stated, turning away and heading inside. "Gonna need some liquor for this."

Before Prescott could make it inside, Seever rested his hand on his shoulder, stopping his progress. "First, how'd you get out?"

Prescott swallowed hard as he hesitated. Then he remembered Nkosi's words, and he grimaced. "Rogan and Sage are lovers. They stop for a quickie whenever they have shifts that overlap."

Seever growled under his breath. "Damn it." Then he turned and headed inside, muttering under his breath, "That means we have a goddamned blind spot that they're using to fuck while on duty."

Alpha Ashton slung his arm over Prescott's shoulders and guided him through the halls. As they walked, he sniffed at him, none-too-discreetly. "Please don't tell me you snuck off the estate to find a fuck," he grumbled. Sniffing again, he groaned, "And with a shifter, too. What the hell, Pres?"

Prescott sat on the end of the sofa, Alpha Ashton next to him. Ranger settled beside Ashton, tugging him away from Prescott. He fought against a smile at the possessive move, wondering if Nkosi would do the same.

"I didn't sneak off the grounds for *just* a fuck," Prescott told them before thanking Reese for the glass of red wine the human handed him. "There were other reasons."

"Such as?" Gilbert asked dryly from where he sat cuddled up beside Hess.

Sighing deeply, Prescott pointed at all the couples around the room—and not just Gilbert and Hess or Ashton and Ranger. Hector sat on Rocky's lap. Thad lounged on another love seat with Lachlan. Cho was being cuddled by Vincentius. While Seever wasn't in the room, Reese and he were fated mates.

"I was feeling lonely and jealous and down," Prescott admitted, feeling a blush heat his cheeks. He took a sip of his wine before running his free hand through his hair. "The walls were starting to close in, like I was in a cage again." Huffing a sigh, Prescott continued, "I know that doesn't make sense, but we used to go out, and now we can't, and it's like —
"

"I get it," Hector piped up, interrupting. "We could go see friends or to a barbeque or visit a restaurant or a park . . . and now we can't." The little scops owl shifter nibbled his bottom lip as he hid his face in Rocky's neck, inhaling deeply.

Gilbert groaned as he nodded slowly. "A gilded cage is still a cage." Then he did something similar, taking comfort in his mate.

"And I didn't have that," Prescott pointed out, waving his hand at all the couples. "And I didn't have a job to keep me busy. No real responsibilities. I was —"

"At loose ends," Ashton murmured, his expression turning pained. "How'd you discover your way out?"

Prescott shrugged. "By accident," he admitted. "I scented Rogan on Sage once when I went to visit Arlon. They're friends." He felt his cheeks grow even hotter as he muttered, "Sage took one look at me at Arlon's door and took off, saying, *have fun*." Prescott rolled his eyes. "Then, I started watching them and discovered their trysts."

Vincentius growled under his breath. "They'll be punished."

"Well, tell 'em the good news that came out of all this," Hess urged with a wide smile on his face.

Gilbert smirked. "You mean besides finding a hole in security?"

"There's actually more," Prescott admitted, unable to stop the smile forming on his lips. After another sip of wine, he admitted, "Nkosi spotted me and gave me this." He held up the flash drive. "Aaaaand" —he paused for dramatic effect, then finished—"we realized we're fated mates."

After several seconds of silence, the room erupted in shouted questions and cries of glee.

CHAPTER FOUR

As much as Nkosi hated to do it, he stood in his small cottage's shower for a good fifteen minutes, scrubbing Prescott's scent from his body. It took several rounds, but he managed it. His skin itched a little, feeling raw, and he lay sprawled on his bed, nude, allowing the sensation to fade.

Lying there, Nkosi's thoughts turned to Prescott. He never would have guessed that following the sexy wood duck shifter would start such a sequence of events. Walking into the club, the other shifter's scent had lingered in the front room, and his dick had thickened.

At the time, Nkosi had attributed it to all the pheromones flooding the club.

Boy, was I wrong.

Thinking of Prescott, his mate, had a predictable impact on his dick . . . namely, he was getting hard.

Nkosi groaned and forced his thoughts to other matters. The flash drive he'd passed along had outlined not only Paraben's location, but the layout of the warehouses they were using. He'd also shared that the ex-councilman intended to stage an attack on Councilman Shane Alvaro's home. The wolf shifter had not only taken over Paraben's seat on the council, but he also had the least protection.

I hope they can rustle up enough protection in time.

Knowing he'd done everything he could that evening, he closed his eyes and let sleep take him.

Heading to the warehouse district, Nkosi pulled his mental

mask around him. He focused on his breathing. As an undercover agent, he had to keep complete control of his emotions so no one ever scented his lies.

Nkosi had been an enforcer for nearly two centuries—first, in his den in South Africa, then when he'd taken up with the council. His job required complete control of his emotions. He carried out duties with swift precision and objectivity.

Emotions could never get in the way.

Somehow, I think that may end up changing.

After only a short time with Prescott, Nkosi felt his need growing. He longed to return to the Vincentius estate. His desire for the other shifter churned in his gut, making his pulse race and sweat break out on his forehead under his helmet.

Gods, stop thinking about him.

Pushing thoughts of his newly discovered and unclaimed mate out of his mind was so much more difficult than Nkosi thought it should be.

No wonder enforcers take jobs close to home once they've mated.

As Nkosi rolled up to the main warehouse, he finally managed to get his pulse back under control. He punched in a code, causing the loading door to lift. Once he had enough clearance, Nkosi started forward.

Nkosi veered to the left, maneuvering around a stack of crates. He knew they were all for show. Once behind them, he took in the lounging area and those in it.

Kennedy sprawled on one end of a sofa with Warsaw on the other. The white rhino and buffalo shifter, respectively, were discussing the upcoming attack. A pair of tiger shifters, Sean and Mindy, sat on another sofa and listened to them.

As soon as Nkosi's motorcycle came into view, they all turned to eye him. He settled his motorcycle on the kickstand, then straightened. After removing his helmet, he placed it on a handlebar.

Nkosi nodded once before swinging off his motorcycle. His

cold mask firmly in place, he strolled across the room to a table set up with a coffee pot and breakfast pastries. He didn't drink coffee, so skipped that. Instead, Nkosi snagged a bear claw and a napkin.

Heading back to the recreation area, Nkosi noticed the unease on Kennedy's face. The rhino glanced around at the others before he shifted in his seat. Nkosi scented that his discomfort was greater than the rest but continued to ignore him as he ate.

Settling on a reclining chair, Nkosi rested his left booted foot on his right knee. He enjoyed his pastry and waited. He knew his silent patience would pay off.

Kennedy cleared his throat and gave Warsaw a pointed look.

Warsaw scowled at his friend.

Finally, Mindy rolled her eyes before focusing on Nkosi. "So, what did you do last night?"

Nkosi arched one brow as he finished chewing his last bite of pastry. "Why?"

He wanted to see what morsels they would drop.

Mindy cocked her head, her blonde hair flowing over her left shoulder. "Because Kennedy is sure he spotted you walking into a gay club last night."

Keeping his breathing steady and his emotions in check, Nkosi licked his fingers, clearing away the traces of the sweet treat. "A gay club?" Arching one brow, Nkosi focused on Kennedy. "While I'm curious why you'd be loitering outside a gay club"—he smirked upon seeing Kennedy's face take on a pinkish glow—"I can assure you, no, I was not enjoying the amenities of a gay club last night."

What Nkosi said was true . . . from a certain point of view. The choice of words always made controlling scent easier. He had not enjoyed any aspect of a gay club, even if he *had* been in one the previous night.

"See." Sean scoffed belligerently. "I told you Nkosi wasn't there." Then the tiger shifter narrowed his eyes at Kennedy. "What were *you* doing there?"

Gotta love the insecurities of bigoted people.

"I was just drivin' by," Kennedy claimed, his voice rising. "I sure as hell didn't stop or nothin'." He waved his hand in Nkosi's direction. "That's why I wasn't sure."

"Well, since we got all that cleared up," Warsaw cut in, his tone dry. "Let's discuss the attack tomorrow." He focused on the tigers. "How many of your pride can we count on?"

Sean and Mindy were alpha and alpha-mate of a tiger pride located in the bayous of Mississippi. They weren't fated, but they shared the same views. One of those was the concept of *might makes right*, and they were both very dominant.

Oh, and they hate homosexuality.

That seems to be a common thread around here.

"Our inner circle, of course," Sean claimed, meaning their beta and three enforcers. "And we can pull a trio of trackers and order a half dozen others. We'll have to leave six of our trackers to make certain those left behind don't make some odd comment to family in other prides."

Mindy nodded. "They'll take them running right after everyone is collected, so they can't talk to anyone."

Kennedy nodded. "Wish I had a pride to get people to help out, but I was a council enforcer for over a century." He shrugged. "No people left." The rhino snapped his fingers. "My friend Gina is sympathetic, though. I bet she would help." Kennedy's expression darkened. "Especially since that asshole, Germaine, accused her of sexual harassment and had her removed from her job as an assistant for Councilman Ridgeston."

"Damn snake shifter is probably gay," Sean snarled, curling his lip. A second later, his eyes widened, and he focused on Nkosi. "Of course, I'm not saying you are." Sean waved his hand in an absent manner. "You bein' a snake and all, too."

Nkosi knew that Germaine was an anaconda shifter. His snake wasn't even in the same ballpark as his own. Germaine was a constrictor, while his own animal wielded an extremely potent venom.

"None taken," Nkosi assured. "And I know nothing about Germaine's sexuality. We don't really run in the same circles."

Snake shifters weren't known to be friendly sorts, even with other snakes.

Prescott popped into his thoughts. His mate was social, sharing his nature with a wood duck. Those animals ran in flocks and were even known to preen each other.

Hmmm . . .

"Well, that snake is an asshole for doing that to Gina," Kennedy continued belligerently. "It was just some harmless flirting."

Nkosi thought Germaine was a fine council enforcer. He also knew it wasn't just *harmless flirting*. Gina hadn't wanted to take no for an answer and had begun touching him inappropriately.

Sexual harassment isn't just done by men.

Upon hearing footsteps coming from down the hall in the back, they all fell silent. Nkosi rose to his feet and headed back to the table in the back. As he picked up another pastry — a powdered sugar-coated, strawberry filled donut — he spotted the ex-councilman approaching.

Two men flanked Paraben.

Recognizing them, Nkosi felt the hairs on the back of his neck stand on end. He set the donut on a plate, then began preparing a cup of tea. After pouring the hot water from a carafe, he opened a teabag containing a satchel of mint medley.

"Ah, Nkosi," Paraben greeted, a wide smile curving his lips. "You're here. Fantastic."

"Good morning, Councilman," Nkosi responded as he

continued to dip his bag. The shifter ordered everyone to address him by that title, even though he no longer was one. "I hear everyone is gearing up for some fun."

"Indeed, we are." Paraben's smile turned predatory. "We'll get some new stock to pass on to our partners." He lifted a hand and indicated the two men behind him. One wore a suit, and the second had on a general's uniform. "You remember Doctor Monren and General Saxx?"

"Of course," Nkosi confirmed, giving each a brief nod. He knew the doctor was actually a bloody scientist, and the general worked out of the army branch of the military. "Good to see you both again."

It really wasn't. They both gave him the creeps. That was probably due to the fact that they'd requested poison samples from his black mamba. No way was that happening, and good thing they didn't know he could poison someone while in human form, too, if he so chose.

"Good, good," Paraben continued. "They're setting up a lab in the back to get those samples from you."

"I see," Nkosi murmured, lifting his cup to his lips. Suddenly, he didn't like the way the pair of men behind the ex-councilman were eyeing his cup. Lowering it a bit, he offered, "Would you care for a cup of tea?"

Both men were very quick to shake their heads and decline. *Too quick.*

And interesting, since he knew the scientist didn't drink coffee.

Nkosi returned the cup to his lips and pretended to take a drink. At the same time, he inhaled deeply. His sensitive shifter nostrils picked up something that shouldn't be there.

A smile twitched at the corners of the scientist's lips.

Hmmm, probably a sedative in the water carafe. Yep, not drinking this.

Picking up his donut plate, Nkosi claimed, "I'd be honored to help our colleagues. I'll be happy to give you my venom, but I do have a request."

"Of course," Doctor Monren immediately replied, his focus shifting between Nkosi and his cup.

Gods, this guy really has no subtlety skills.

"I'll need to give it to you after tomorrow's attack on the wolf and his family." When Nkosi saw the doctor's frown and Paraben begin to cross his arms, he gave his leader a cold smile. "I've been storing my venom for weeks in anticipation of us making a move." His chuckle sounded rusty and mean. "I don't want to run short during the battle by donating right beforehand."

Paraben's green eyes widened, and he began to nod. His smile appeared malicious.

Perfect.

"Of course," Paraben responded. "That would be extremely short-sided of me." Turning his attention to the scientist, who didn't appear happy, Paraben continued, "Tomorrow is important, after all. We're acquiring new specimens for you."

Gods, specimens. I hate this shifter.

Before Doctor Monren could respond, Paraben turned back to Nkosi. "Come." He flailed his hand as if indicating the lounging area. "Let's discuss—"

His hand hit Nkosi's teacup, and he didn't even try to hold onto it. He let it fall. The paper cup spilled his drink all over the cement floor of the warehouse, splashing across all their pant legs in the process.

General Saxx growled and took a step backward, looking annoyed.

"Ah, so sorry, so sorry," Paraben lied, peering at the floor. "Come on." He led them away from the mess, not even bothering to clean it up. "I'll get a fresh pot of water for you in a few minutes. I need your thoughts on something first."

A glance out of the corner of his eye showed Nkosi that the scientist sported a red face and narrowed eyes.

Well, fuck. I hadn't wanted to believe what I'd overheard. It seems the good ex-councilman is willing to sell his own people if the price is right. Damn. Time to take this guy out.

CHAPTER FIVE

"Why would you ask to go to Shane's," Jared Templeton asked, arching one brow. His cool tone held a note of curiosity.

Jared had arrived that morning, along with his wolf shifter mate, Carson Angeni. They'd been flown in from Stone Ridge, Colorado by another wolf enforcer, Manon Lemelle. They'd been accompanied by Beta Dixon Holsteen and a few other volunteers who'd wanted to help their ex-beta—Shane Alvaro.

Prescott had heard that Carson would be changing his name to Kajika at some point, but it wouldn't happen until after he returned to Stone Ridge. So far, he hadn't heard about Jared's new name. He figured they would decide on it eventually.

"Nkosi will be there," Prescott admitted. "I want to do something to help him stay safe."

Ashton rested his hand on Prescott's shoulder. "But you're not a fighter, Pres." He glanced around and added, "None of us are."

"You don't have to be a fighter to help," Jared pointed out from where he leaned his back against Carson. "There are other ways to fight."

Hess snorted. "Are you quoting from *Captain America* now, Jared?" Grinning widely, the big bear shifter waggled his brows. "Thought you'd be more of an *Iron Man* guy, him bein' a rich vigilante type fella and all."

Jared chuckled and shook his head. "*Captain American* runs

around in tight clothes, while *Iron Man* is in a metal suit." Waggling his brows, he added, "Now tell me which one you think I would prefer."

Barking a laugh, Hess lifted both hands in surrender.

While Carson shook his head, Jared continued, "And while it is similar to the line in the movie, it's not verbatim." Then he hummed, his expression turning just a smidge vacant. "Although that red, white, and blue outfit he wore on stage was definitely . . . mmmm."

"Behave, love," Carson ordered with a smile and a nip to Jared's neck. "Tell them your thoughts." Jared's grin lit up his hazel eyes, and Carson quickly added, "In regards to the battle tomorrow evening."

Jared turned his head and peered over his shoulder at Carson. "Spoilsport." When Carson just smirked at his mate, Jared refocused on the group. "I'm saying, you're fliers. If you want to help, there are a number of things you can do."

"Such as?" Prescott twisted his fingers together in anticipation. He wanted to be there for his mate.

Anything to help end this.

"Well, you can carry ammunition to those who are using weapons," Jared began slowly. "Such as myself while I lie on the roof and pick off our enemy. Not like I'm going to want to get down."

"Me, either."

While Jared lifted both brows, he didn't look entirely surprised by the black-haired man's appearance. The guy's dark eyes held a definite gleam of mischief. Over one shoulder, he had slung a fancy-looking rifle. His other arm was wrapped around a pale-skinned, pointy-chinned male who smelled like a fox. The stranger scented heavily of sage and moss.

"How the fuck did you get in here?" Seever snarled, advancing slowly. He bristled with obvious irritation. "Who are you?"

"His name is Raven," Carson stated, growling softly. "And

40

what *are* you doing here?"

"I contacted him." Another man stated, coming into the quickly filling recreation room, although this one was being led into the room by Johnnie, one of Seever's men. Several others filed in behind them. His hazel eyes held a gleam of disapproval as he stared at Raven. "You should have just come in with us, however."

"Alpha Kontra," Carson greeted with a dip of his head. "Good to see you again."

"And you, Carson," Alpha Kontra replied. Then he turned to Councilman Goldstein. "Thank you for allowing my people and I into your home, Councilman." The huge shifter — a grizzly bear, if Prescott remembered correctly — dipped his head. "I look forward to helping your people clear out the riff-raff."

After Vincentius returned Alpha Kontra's greeting, he peered around at all the humans and shifters filling the space. "Thank you all for heeding my call. *I* am the one who's honored." He lifted a hand before anyone could say anything. "Although, I do understand that your support has more to do with the threat to Councilman Alvaro."

"Actually, it's because Paraben is still teaming up with scientists," Raven revealed before flopping onto a chair. He tugged the fox shifter onto his lap. "I received a note on an old message board I used to use to communicate with Marlow."

A variety of cries erupted not only from Prescott, but many of his flock-mates. Hector and Cho clung to their lovers, while growls erupted from Ashton, Gilbert, and Thad. Prescott hunched in on himself, wishing he had his own mate there to hold him.

Ashton reached over and grasped his shoulder in support.

Unable to help himself, Prescott turned and pressed his face against his alpha's chest. While Ashton rubbed up and down his back, Ranger reached over and squeezed his upper arm. Relief filled him that his alpha's mate wasn't asking him to move.

"Quiet!" Vincentius roared, causing silence to fall over the room. He pointed at Raven. "Let's try this again. Your name is Raven, and you just admitted to working with the scientists. Give us one good reason we shouldn't lock you up right now."

Raven smirked, looking completely unconcerned. The man sitting on his lap didn't look nearly as unaffected. Instead, he growled fiercely at the councilman.

"Relax, Liam," Raven murmured, nuzzling the pale man's temple. "We may be here to help, but we're outsiders. Remember, my mate?"

"Mate?" Seever glanced between them, then scented the air. After rolling his eyes, he flopped into another chair before waving his hand. "There's plenty of space. Will everyone get comfortable? I can imagine there'll need to be a few explanations."

After a bit of milling around, during which Reese, Rocky, and Johnnie began passing out drinks, most everyone was seated.

"So, yes," Raven began after a sip of his rum. "I used to work for Marlow. He altered me, enhancing some of my abilities." With a wave of his hand, he added, "I'll explain that later. Suffice it to say, it's why I smell a little off." He pointed at a dirty-blond-haired man. "That's Ryan. He was altered, too."

"Ryan's mated with my beta, Sam," Kontra told everyone.

"Right. Anyway," Raven continued. "I realized Marlow's vendetta against shifters was bullshit. I admit I was just gonna walk away, but then I found my mate amongst the shifters being held at Marlow's facility, and I needed help busting him and the others out." Cupping Liam's jaw, Raven smiled at the man. "I warned you I'm not a very good man."

Liam's look was so full of love that it made Prescott's gut churn with longing. "You're good enough for me."

While Raven lowered his head and sealed his lips over Liam's in a slow make-out session, Carson picked up the tale. "Raven came to us, since we'd had prior dealings with him."

Prescott could only guess at what those were, and he wasn't certain he wanted to know, considering the growl in Carson's tone.

"So, Raven and Ryan, who was Raven's inside man, helped us clear out Marlow's facility, and he took off with Liam. They ended up settling in a lion pride in Kansas." Carson shrugged. "Anyway, we eventually caught Marlow. In the meantime, Ryan went north and helped Kontra's people clear a different facility, mating with Sam in the process."

"We've cleared out every facility we can find," Jared told everyone. "Saving and rehabilitating any shifter we could."

"Like us," Ashton murmured. "We are grateful."

Prescott gathered himself and straightened on the sofa.

"Anyway, I was contacted." Raven must have finished his lip-lock at some point. "So I'm here to help stop another one. I contacted Ryan, and he and Kontra's men joined us."

Jared chuckled coldly. "Thanks for joining the party." He waggled his brows. "Now we'll have enough people to not only defend Shane's place, but clear out the warehouses." Rubbing his palms together with a gleeful smile on his face, Jared murmured, "This'll be so much fun."

"Only you," Dixon commented with a roll of his eyes. He pulled a toothpick out of his shirt pocket and pointed it at Jared. "You taking charge or letting the councilman have a say?" Then he stuck the wooden stick into his mouth.

His lips curving into a feral smile, Jared pinned a gaze on Raven. "Actually, I figured I'd work with the ex-military on this one."

Ryan lifted both brows. "Uh, I'm a sniper," he reminded everyone. "I pretty much point and shoot whoever my superiors tell me to, sooooo . . ."

Raven sighed deeply. "I will assist." Then he pointed at Seever. "With him at our side. Your security is good. We should go over Shane's together."

"You still managed to beat it," Seever pointed out, sounding disgruntled. "Gonna tell me how?"

"Of course," Raven replied. His expression softened as he glanced around at Prescott and his flock-mates. "Can't have the scientists managing to reacquire these guys."

Seever growled. "Damn straight."

"So, what does everyone say we move this party to the formal dining room?" Reese asked from where he stood in the doorway. "It's lunchtime and chows on." He began mouthing words as he pointed at everyone in the room in turn.

Prescott realized he was counting.

As everyone started rising from their seats, Reese nodded. "Yeah. I have enough plates set." Then he froze as the blood drained from his face. "Oh, gods. Please tell me no one has any food allergies or special dietary needs."

Wrapping his arm around Reese's waist, Seever drew his mate to his side. "Everyone is good, babe. Just relax."

Reese peered up at Seever, his expression earnest. "But how do you know? Did you ask?"

"I'm allergic to peanuts," Miach stated, raising his hand.

Next, Cho perked up. "Are you serving *SpaghettiOs*?"

Jared smirked. "I really hate most melons."

Rubbing the back of his neck, Ryan revealed, "Uh, I'm allergic to shellfish."

"Is that why you always stop kissing me for an hour when I eat clams?" Sam asked, clearly shocked. When Ryan nodded, Sam groaned and clutched him close. "Damn it, mate. You should have said something. I don't have to eat them."

"But you love clam strips or sautéed oysters or steamed lobster or shrimp" — Ryan snickered as he finished — "any way you can get it."

Sam moaned and licked his lips, obviously thinking about all the food Ryan had just listed. Then his eyes widened, and he met his mate's grinning gaze. His cheeks flushed.

Petting Sam's broad chest, Ryan murmured, "You love your seafood. It's fine."

"I'll brush my teeth right after," Sam vowed.

Ryan grinned. "Okay."

"Okay, soooo . . ." Reese glanced around the group. He pointed at Cho. "Sorry. I'll get your *SpaghettiOs* on the menu for dinner." Then he pointed at Miach. "Stay away from the broccoli salad. There's shaved peanuts in it to give it a crunch." Finally, Reese pointed at Ryan. "Don't touch the jambalaya soup."

Then Reese turned and started out of the recreation room.

"Hey," Jared called. "What about me? No melon on the table today?"

Reese paused and peered over his shoulder. Scoffing, he looked Jared up and down as he curled his lip. "Uh, you're a big boy. You know what melon looks like in fruit salad." Turning away, Reese continued out of the room as he grumbled, "Besides, it's not like it's an allergy or something."

Prescott turned his attention back to Jared. For an instant, he took in the shocked expression on the human's face. Then the man tipped his head back and laughed heartily.

Ashton wrapped his arm around Prescott, and with his other arm around Ranger, he guided them both out of the room.

Once Prescott settled at the table, he realized the huge formal dining room was filled to capacity. It was a good thing not everyone in Dixon's pack and Kontra's gang had descended on the estate. That was partly due to the fact that they were trying to hide their numbers.

Maybe that's why Raven snuck in.

Speaking of Raven, the altered human had settled next to Seever. He was busy putting food on both Liam's plate as well as his own. At the same time, he explained how he'd snuck not only onto the estate grounds but into the mansion without detection.

At least it didn't involve Rogan this time.

The poor lion shifter had received quite the dressing down from Seever . . . or so Prescott had heard. He hadn't actually been there. So had Sage, for that matter.

According to rumors, the pair had been so guilt-riddled, they'd broken up.

Prescott felt horrible about that. He tried to keep in mind that they weren't fated mates, but for a few hours, he'd contemplated how to reunite them. Since they weren't mates, he wasn't certain if that was for the best.

Something to think upon another time.

After Prescott loaded his bowl with jambalaya and his plate with stuffed peppers and sides, he turned his attention to his food. Flavors exploded across his tongue, and he sighed happily. Prescott relished the fruit salad—he loved melons—as well as everything else he could stuff into his belly.

I hope Nkosi is eating okay.

Prescott didn't have any idea what kind of food the ex-councilman had access to. Thinking of his mate, he remembered a question that hadn't been fully answered. He turned his attention to Jared, who was busy demolishing a bowl of jambalaya.

"Jared?" Prescott called tentatively.

After shoving his spoonful of food into his mouth, Jared turned his attention on Prescott. In lieu of speaking with his mouth full, the human arched one brow in obvious question.

"What other way could I help at Shane's tomorrow?" Then he glanced around and waved his hand to indicate his flock-mates. "Or others, if they're interested."

Ryan answered. "I heard you're fliers, right?"

Prescott nodded.

"So take people medical supplies," Ryan offered. "Bandages, ointment, and the like. Or keep an eye on the battlefield and let our medics know where people need help." He grinned widely. "Can you imagine our medic racing after a flock of birds?"

Kontra spoke up next. "If one of you wants to link up with one of our warlocks, we could get two aerial views instead of one."

"You have warlocks in your gang?" Vincentius sounded shocked, his fork pausing halfway to his mouth.

"We do," Kontra confirmed. "A crow, too. Castor. He's linked up with a warlock before on a mission." He shrugged with a wistful smile. "All our other fliers stayed with Dorian and his flock south of Albuquerque."

"I'll do it." Gilbert lifted his hand. "I'll call out patterns and sneak attacks."

Kontra grinned. "Good."

Jared cleared his throat. "I suppose those are worthy tasks."

Carson heaved a sigh even as he threaded his fingers through Jared's ear-length, shaggy locks. "And what were you thinking, love?"

With a shrug and a grin, Jared told them, "They could drop grenades on the enemy."

CHAPTER SIX

Nkosi knew what Paraben expected him to do—slither around the battlefield and bite any shifter opposing their side. While he'd agreed, he hadn't told the ex-councilman that he would need to scent each and every person on their side—shifter and human alike—in order to know friend from foe. No way was he shifting to snake form around the military personal that General Saxx was providing.

Gods, baby. Please have your people come together enough to defend against thirty-plus shifters and a hundred soldiers.

When Nkosi had created the encrypted drive, he hadn't realized there would be so many. He'd thought maybe a couple dozen would join the shifters' ranks. Evidently, the general wanted to recreate several of the installations that had been destroyed by shifters and vampires over the years.

Now I just have to figure out how to help the others without blowing my cover, too.

After that thought, another popped into his head.

No way am I going to get out of blowing my cover this time around. I just can't do it.

Nkosi decided a call to Councilman Goldstein was in order. "Well," he murmured, rising to his feet. "I'm going to go get laid this afternoon before the fight later." Upon seeing a number of shocked expressions, he smirked while popping his neck. "Need to pound some pussy and blow off steam."

"What?" Kennedy appeared completely shocked.

Warsaw snorted. "Have fun, man."

While Sean smirked, Mindy scowled.

Uncaring, Nkosi started out of the lounge in the warehouse.

"Nkosi!" Paraben called. "Where are you going?"

Damn. I'd hoped to make a clean break.

Nkosi didn't bother stopping. He swung his leg over his motorcycle seat before picking up his helmet. While sliding it over his head, Nkosi replied to the shifter.

"I'm going to a bar to pick up some lady to fuck," Nkosi stated calmly.

He'd learned long ago that the more vulgar he was, the quicker Paraben would get away from him. Even though the asshat sold shifters to humans to be experimented on, he still considered himself a gentleman.

Fucker.

"You can't leave now," Paraben countered, grabbing one of his handlebars. "Everyone needs to stay here. Just in case."

Ignoring Paraben's hold, Nkosi fired up his motorcycle. "Just in case?"

"Um, well—"

Hmmm. Did the man have suspicions of a plant?

Nkosi sighed noisily. "Look, Councilman. I'm about to go into battle for our cause." He wished the man could see his face so he could paste a lecherous smile on his lips. Instead, he allowed his tone to turn husky with need as he reached down and palmed his crotch. "If I'm gonna die, I'm gonna make sure my bone gets waxed one last time before that happens."

Just as Nkosi had hoped, Paraben jerked back.

Good.

Nkosi took the opportunity to click his motorcycle into gear. As he held the brake for the front wheel and revved his engine, he flipped the kickstand up. In the next instant, he tilted his bike and swung his rear tire around.

To Nkosi's pleasure, the ex-councilman leaped backward.

He took the opportunity to holler, "See you all later for a different kind of fun." His laugh sounded harsh, even to himself. He hollered, "Can't wait to clear out some ass-lickers and their friends." As Nkosi squealed his tires and rocketed out of the warehouse, he swallowed back the bile threatening to rise up his throat.

This was so much easier when I didn't have to worry about my words and actions getting back to my mate.

Once clear of the building, Nkosi headed into town. He weaved through traffic, checking his mirrors often. After making certain he wasn't being followed, he steered his motorcycle back out of town.

Nkosi made his way into the foothills west of the city. Finding the parking area he wanted, he headed along the drive. He parked, turned off his bike, and removed his helmet.

After locking that on the motorcycle's back hook, Nkosi hurried up the hiking path. He easily found the hollow tree he wanted. Reaching in, he pulled out a small satchel.

Returning to the edge of the clearing, Nkosi made certain he had a signal on his burner phone while staying amidst the trees. Then he made his call. He leaned against a tree, waiting for Vincentius to pick up.

A phone call was always a risk, but he knew this time he had no choice—hence staying in the trees, just in case.

"This is Vincentius."

"Nkosi here."

Vincentius scoffed. "Hello, Prescott's mate."

Sighing, Nkosi couldn't help but ask, "How is he?"

"Missing you."

For some reason, that information caused a flutter in his gut. While he didn't want his mate to hurt, he liked that he missed him. Hell, he missed his duck, too.

"Tell him I feel the same."

Vincentius hummed. "Will do, but that's not why you're calling."

"No," Nkosi confirmed. "There are far more humans than anticipated, provided by the general." He hesitated, then admitted, "I don't think I can keep my cover intact with so many."

"You won't need to."

Nkosi's lips parted at Vincentius's surprising response.

Evidently, Nkosi remained quiet too long, for Vincentius asked, "Did you hear me?"

"I did," Nkosi confirmed, getting his head out of his ass. "May I ask why?"

Hell, he'd been deep-cover for over a year and a half. The councilman had always appreciated and encouraged more reports. Why was he saying it would no longer be needed?

"Let's just say, we have plenty of extra on our side, too," Vincentius told him, pleasure filling his tone. "So, how many humans? What's their abilities?"

"Abilities?" Nkosi wasn't certain what the councilman meant. "They're . . . military."

"Ah, so not enhanced."

Nkosi frowned. "What the hell does that mean?"

Vincentius chuckled softly. "A lot has happened here, my friend."

Friend? Since when?

Sighing, Vincentius murmured, "The initial scientist, Marlow, figured out how to enhance humans. We have a few of them on our side, compliments of Shane's contacts."

"Oh, damn," Nkosi whispered, unable to help himself. "That's . . . unexpected."

"We're clearing their warehouses at the same time as their attack on Shane, so you just do the best you can to stay safe. Help if you can, but don't put your life on the line."

Nkosi gaped, unable to think of a response to that order.

"You know you're going to be living here after this, Nkosi," Vincentius continued, obviously realizing his quiet stemmed from his confusion. "Prescott is your mate, and his flock lives here. That's where you'll end up, too."

Give up his solitary cabin in the foothills?

"I'll build you and Prescott something, but he's a duck."

"Gods, it's like you keep reading my mind," Nkosi grumbled, rubbing his palm over his nearly shorn scalp. "It's fucking weird, Councilman."

Vincentius chuckled softly. "You'll get used to it." After clearing his throat, he added, "Anything else we need to know?"

"I'm in position at seven-thirty this evening, but they plan to attack at shift change."

"Ah, so eight-fifteen then," Vincentius mused. "Meaning they intend to get there early enough to see if any extra people are placed."

"Right."

Nkosi could practically see the councilman nodding his head as he muttered, "We'll be in place well before then."

"Good." Nkosi hesitated, then couldn't help but ask, "You're keeping Prescott safe?" The longer Vincentius remained quiet, the more dread filled Nkosi. "Councilman?"

Vincentius sighed deeply. "He and several other fliers want to help," he revealed, sounding frustrated. "They'll be carrying ammunition, doing reconnaissance, and a couple of other tasks that only someone flying can do."

Nkosi groaned roughly, resting his forehead in his free palm. "Oh, gods, but there's guns." He couldn't remember the last time he'd whined, but the sound was in his voice right then. "Tell them there's guns. Lots of them. They can't take to the open air, or they'll be shot."

The idea of bullets slamming into Prescott's pretty little wood duck body—not that he'd had a chance to see it, yet— filled his mind, and for the first time in over a century, his body broke into a cold sweat as fear saturated him.

"Hey! Hey!" Vincentius called. "Nkosi. Nkosi. Listen to me."

While Nkosi had no idea how long Vincentius had been talking, he finally dragged his brain back online. He shook his head once, then swallowed hard. After a second and third gulp, he gathered enough moisture to speak.

"Sorry," Nkosi rasped. "I'm here. Shit." He had no idea if or when he'd ever had a panic attack before. "I'm okay." While Nkosi wasn't totally certain of that, he knew he would have to be. "Just, um, warn them all to stay safe." After all, it wasn't just Prescott up there. Other fliers would be involved, too. "Wing between trees, and do the best they can to zig-zag and shit."

"I'll tell them, and now I'm telling this to you. If you see a blue light highlighting your area, you have ten seconds to clear it."

Huh.

"Okay." Spotting another vehicle entering the trailhead parking area, Nkosi narrowed his eyes. He recognized it. "Gotta go."

"Stay safe," the councilman encouraged.

"You all, too." Then Nkosi disconnected. He quickly placed the phone into his satchel as he watched Warsaw get out of the car. "Now what the hell are you doing here?"

Heading back up the trail, Nkosi made swift, silent work of stashing his phone and bag. He strode into a nearby clearing next. Lying down, he unbuttoned his jeans, placed one hand behind his head, and shoved the other into his pants.

Slowly tugging on his damn near unresponsive dick, Nkosi waited for the other man to hike up the trail and sniff him out.

It didn't take long.

Warsaw paused in the small clearing off to the side of the trail. His eyes narrowed as he took in his reclining form. His jaw clenched as he peered around the area.

"Odd," Warsaw muttered.

"Oh?" Nkosi glanced down at where he continued to fondle himself under the cover of his jeans. "I'm pretty sure you do this on a regular basis, too."

Shrugging, Warsaw shoved his hands into his pockets. "Sure, but you said you were gonna pick up some pussy." He made a big production of looking around. "I don't see any chicks around here. Do you?"

Nkosi growled as he fixed a glare on Warsaw. "Seriously? Why the fuck would I want to spend the last couple of hours before my life is in danger, trolling in a goddamned bar."

Warsaw pulled his hands out of his pockets so he could cross them over his chest. "Because you said you were going to." The buffalo shifter lifted his broad shoulders in a shrug. "I was gonna join you. Wanted that kind of stress relief, too."

"Well, sorry to disappoint." Nkosi cocked his head and stared at the other shifter. He knew he could shift and drop the other male with his venom before Warsaw had even completed his change, so he decided he was safe enough to ask, "So, how did you find me?"

Huffing a sigh, Warsaw strolled toward him slowly. "You're being tracked." He bent his knees and settled cross-legged ten feet to Nkosi's left. "Paraben plans to sell you to that fucking scientist."

Surprised upon hearing the malice dripping from Warsaw's tone, Nkosi eased his hand out of his jeans. He took a moment to button them up, keeping a narrow-eyed gaze on the other shifter. Finally, he rocked to a sitting position, turning on his butt and folding his legs to mirror the much larger male.

"Why?" Nkosi drew the word out. "Why would you tell me this?"

Curling his lip, Warsaw growled low in his throat. He flicked his gaze to Nkosi, then peered around the trees. Finally, he cocked his head and acted as if he were listening intently.

"I watched you drive up," Nkosi shared, realizing what the

man was trying to discern.

Are we alone?

Warsaw's eyes widened. He flicked his attention to Nkosi's groin, then back to his face. Even his jaw worked with obvious discomfort.

Odd.

Nkosi waved a hand in a *go ahead* motion, annoyed at being followed even though he was interested in what the buffalo shifter had to say.

"Okay, I'm gonna tell you something, but if you ever repeat it to anyone, I'll totally deny it." Warsaw glared at him, lifting a thick finger and pointing it at him. "And I'll figure out how to do that shit where you scent like you're telling the truth, even when you're not."

Huh. Interesting.

"If it makes you feel better, I figured out yesterday that Paraben intends to allow the scientists to study me, whether through selling or not." Nkosi figured that wasn't too much to admit to. "And the shifter's an asshole." Shaking his head, he hardened his features. "Selling our kind to humans so humans can give our gifts to their soldiers. Fucking greedy bastard."

"What?" Warsaw's eyes widened. "What did you say?"

Nkosi snorted. "Oh, did you actually think this was about his hatred of gays?" Rolling one shoulder, he admitted, "My snake can curl up pretty tight, and there are *sooo* many nooks and crannies in those warehouses. I hear all sorts of things."

Warsaw gaped at him for a few seconds, then snapped his mouth shut. His brows furrowed. "Why are you admitting this to me?"

Barking a laugh, Nkosi curled his lip. "You followed me out here to . . . what?" He waved his hand around the area. "If you ended up a threat, I could knock you out long enough for you to miss the attack. Then I could tell everyone that *you're* a spy." Smirking at the huge blond, Nkosi leaned forward, resting his forearms on his knees. "Well, Warsaw? What the fuck is up with you?"

"I-I-I . . . I'm gay," Warsaw barked out. "And I know you're gay."

Well, that certainly hadn't been what Nkosi had expected. "Another odd thing to admit right now, but I'm actually bisexual."

Warsaw's cheeks darkened, but he forged ahead anyhow. "I can't believe I let Kennedy talk me into this shit, but he's been my best friend for decades." His blue eyes gleamed as sadness creased his expression. "But I can't do this. I know you're in contact with Vincentius. I thought maybe you could help me get out of this mess."

Well, fuck a duck.

Realizing what he'd just thought, he fought back a smile. His blood flowed south.

Now is not the time to be thinking of Prescott.

"You don't believe me," Warsaw murmured, bobbing his head while furrowing his brows. "I'll prove it. You said you're bi."

Nkosi was too distracted by thoughts of his mate to follow Warsaw's ramblings, so he completely missed the bigger man moving. When the buffalo shifter shoved him backward, *that* drew his attention. He began to shuffle away from him, preparing to shift, when he felt Warsaw's hands on his fly, and he froze.

In shock, Nkosi watched as Warsaw inhaled the scent of his arousal. The other shifter's moan caused the hairs on his thighs to stand on end. Then Warsaw started unbuttoning his fly, but that didn't make him harden. Instead, Nkosi began to soften.

"Shit," Nkosi hissed. "Stop." He gripped Warsaw's shoulders and pushed even as he shifted his hips away from the male. "Warsaw, stop now."

Warsaw obeyed, lifting his head. While arousal poured from the buffalo shifter, he did as ordered. He peered up at him with slightly glassy eyes.

"You need to stop now, Warsaw," Nkosi ordered softly, disentangling him from the other man. "I can't do this."

Rocking onto his knees, Warsaw sported such a confused expression. It appeared so strange on the big male's face. "But, you said you're bi."

"I've also met my mate," Nkosi revealed. The words were out of his mouth before he could think better of them.

Shit.

Warsaw blinked once, twice. Then his expression cleared. "Oh. Oh, wow," he murmured. Lifting his hands, he rocked back onto his ass. "I'm sorry. I never would have touched you if I'd known. I—" Warsaw scowled as he returned his huge hands to his thighs. His cheeks were damn near scarlet. "Sorry."

"Don't apologize." Nkosi sighed deeply. One thing he knew for sure now, though, Warsaw was definitely gay. "Why come to me now? You want out? Walk away. Go to your councilman and tell him everything."

Wincing, Warsaw shook his head. "I'll end up being doped up by Enforcer Delanrue and having my brain picked clean."

"Sure that's not a great thing to look forward to," Nkosi admitted. "But it could be worse."

Warsaw scoffed harshly. "What's worse than admitting you love a man when you know that guy is listening and already mated?"

Nkosi gaped. He hadn't expected that. "Um."

"Yeah." Warsaw shook his head. "And I'm not telling who." He scrubbed his hands through his hair. "I'll get over it eventually. Maybe I'll meet my mate, and everything will be better."

Sighing deeply, Nkosi thought swiftly. With the way Warsaw was spilling his guts, he realized a couple of things. One, the buffalo shifter really was gay. Two, he was terrified to go into a battle that he didn't have the heart to fight.

Meeting Warsaw's gaze, Nkosi stared intently at him. "Warsaw, don't go to your assigned location this evening."

"What?" The buffalo shifter appeared so confused.

Nkosi grabbed his forearm. "Don't. Go." His eyes narrowed the more Warsaw's eyes widened. "Hole up in my cottage until I come get you." Nkosi held up the keys to his sanctuary. "Stay there. I'm going to use your absence to help my own cause."

Warsaw took the keys ever-so-slowly. "Really?"

Nodding once, Nkosi smirked. "You did say you knew I was the spy. You want out, I'll help you with that, and we'll both capitalize on your desertion." He shrugged. "Plus, I'll put in a good word for you."

"Th-Thanks."

Nkosi nodded again. He didn't tell the other shifter that his place was wired for video and sound, so he would know if Warsaw betrayed him.

CHAPTER SEVEN

"Movement in sector three."

The voice came in over the speaker embedded in the headband strapped around Prescott's duck head. They hadn't been certain it would work, but after testing it on each of the fliers who'd volunteered, they'd discovered it did. Their avian auditory systems easily made out the whispered words.

Prescott knew sector three was Ashton's area. His own was sector five. There were five in all, ringing around Shane's home. Thad waited in the trees of sector one. Each of them had three grenades in their nests.

Jared and Ryan were on the roof of the home, preparing to shoot a set of charges in sectors two and four. The human planned to use the initial blasts to cause chaos and take out as many as possible. Prescott would have felt bad about blowing people up, but he knew if these guys won, there was a very high probability that he would end up back in a cage.

Never again.

"Movement in sector two." The voice belonged to Draven, a warlock linked with Gilbert.

Worry for his beta filled Prescott. The raven had the most dangerous job. He was winging his way over the trees as if searching for food. Instead, Draven was looking through Gilbert's eyes, allowing him to call out where their intruders were.

"Movement in all sectors now," Draven told everyone. "They're at the gray line."

"Turn on the blue lights in fifteen seconds," Jared ordered.

"Volley on my count."

Prescott's heart hammered in his chest. It was beginning. He placed his webbed foot on the grenade, preparing to pull the pin.

Please don't get injured. Please don't get injured.

While the news from Vincentius that Nkosi was missing him had warmed Prescott, he feared for his mate. His snake was down there somewhere, coming in through sector one. He'd wanted to be the one in that area, but Ashton and Jared had kyboshed it. They'd worried he would hesitate, trying to confirm his mate was clear.

Prescott had accepted that they were most likely right.

A blue glow popped up in the area below him. Lights with blue bulbs had been buried beneath the leaves. The cover created an eerie effect.

"Fire in four, three, two, one."

When Jared finished counting down, Prescott jerked his head up, yanking out the pin. Then he carefully gripped the grenade in his bill and tossed it as far as he could to his left. It flew out of the tree and out of sight.

Prescott swiftly did the same to his second grenade, throwing that to the right. His third grenade was tossed forward, away from the councilman's home. The explosions began before the third one was out of sight.

Hunkering down in his nest, Prescott waited until the third explosion. Dirt, leaves, smoke, and things he didn't plan to look at too closely flew up all around him. He trembled as his tree shook beneath him.

When Prescott heard a crack and an even harsher shudder rock him, he knew he couldn't stay. Ignoring the shouts of surprise, the cries of agony, and the pop of gunfire, Prescott spread his wings. It wasn't easy for a duck to fly out of a tree, but with the adrenaline surging through him, he did it.

Flapping swiftly, Prescott climbed higher. He knew better than to break tree cover unless he absolutely had to, so he zipped around the upper branches. His blood thudded through his veins as he poured on as much speed as he could.

Prescott spotted the small mansion in the distance, and relief began to seep into him, calming his frayed nerves. All the fliers were supposed to head to a third-story turret. The windows were open, allowing them to return to the safety of the home.

Just as Prescott reached the roof's edge, pain slashed through his left wing. He honked in surprise, and his initial reaction was to pull his wing in protectively. His flight faltered for a second before he fought through the pain.

Unfortunately, Prescott couldn't maintain altitude. He descended swiftly, and he braced for impact. The scrape of the shingles over his feathers, as well as the jolt from hitting the roof, sent a new kind of pain through him.

Prescott's body rolled and tumbled, and he lost his sense of direction. Spreading his right wing, he tried to stop the momentum. He smacked into a wall and hoped it was for the turret. When he immediately started rolling in the other direction, Prescott knew he was right.

Too bad the pain surging through his body caused spots to dance across his vision, and he couldn't seem to catch his balance.

"Gotcha."

Prescott honked in surprise. His first response was to peck and struggle.

"Relax, Prescott."

Recognizing the voice as Ryan's, Prescott slumped.

"There ya go, little buddy," Ryan muttered. "Almost there. Here."

Prescott managed to blink the spots out of his eyes as Ryan's hands disappeared, and he was placed in someone else's grip. He saw Caroline's concerned expression—Councilman Shane Alvaro's mate. Honking softly, he tried to reassure her. When she smiled, Prescott hoped it had worked.

"I'm back to my post," Ryan stated, then slipped across the roof.

"You'll be fine now, Prescott," Caroline assured as she turned away from the window. "You'll be pleased to hear that you're the last one in."

Sighing, Prescott nodded his head a little. That *was* good news.

"The break in sector four is an official retreat," Jared grumbled through the speaker. "Where the fuck is Bashir? With his speed, he should be stopping them easy."

"Oh, stop your whining." Bashir sounded amused. "Lachlan needed an assist. I'm on 'em."

"I did *not* need an assist," Lachlan countered. The wildcat shifter had been leading a group to clear sector five. "There was just a lag because Ryan was otherwise occupied."

Bashir cackled in response.

Damn. He's enjoying this way too much.

Prescott had always found the vampire friendly and fun-loving. He'd taught them to ballroom dance with his buddy Arlon. On the battlefield, he seemed like a completely different person.

I suppose that makes sense. I never would have thought I'd throw grenades at soldiers.

"Okay," Caroline murmured. "Just settle here. Give me this."

Caroline placed Prescott on a pillow in a large room that had been turned into the command center. From the rearranged furniture, he guessed it had been an entertainment and living space. He didn't fight Caroline as she eased his headband off of him.

Immediately, Prescott began to shift.

"Prescott. Not, yet."

Prescott ignored Caroline's warning and pushed through

his change. By the time he resumed his human form, he was panting hard. Sweat beaded on his forehead, and the skin on his left arm burned. Black spots danced across his vision once more.

Caroline sighed deeply as she gripped one leg.

He couldn't even dredge up any embarrassment as the councilman's mate helped him into a pair of sweatpants.

"Let's take a look at that arm," Caroline murmured, gripping his wrist lightly.

"It's just a graze," Prescott assured, finally gathering himself. "I've had worse." He peered at his bleeding arm. "Nothing's broken. I know what that feels like."

Caroline hummed as she grabbed some first aid supplies. "While I'm sorry you know what broken bones feel like" — she began cleaning his arm—"I do believe you're right."

"Why am I in here and not the medical suites upstairs?" Prescott couldn't contain his curiosity. The dozen bedrooms upstairs had all been turned into make-shift triage rooms. "Why were you in the turret?"

"I was their back-up plan in case something like what happened to you took place," Caroline explained. Then she pointed at the monitor to his left. "And I thought you'd want to see that."

The monitor showed sector one . . . where Nkosi should have entered the premises. Judging by the dropping shifters, he had, too. Except, he wasn't taking out Shane's people, but his own, declaring his true allegiance.

Prescott's heart thudded in his chest for a whole new reason. His mate would be coming home with him tonight. They could truly be together.

Then a massive white rhinoceros began doing an odd stomping dance. His front feet thudded back and forth, and Prescott imagined he could feel the tremors from there. He felt his heart rate speed up as he realized what the shifter must have been trying to do — *stomp my mate.*

Three lions converged on the rhino, drawing the big beast's attention.

Fear caused Prescott to draw closer to the monitor, ignoring Caroline's ministrations. He squinted his eyes, staring into the grass. Between the darkness and the fact that the camera was so far away, he knew it was useless, but he had to try.

A second later, a large raven swooped onto the screen. He snatched something on the ground and soared back into the air. His wings spread, he veered toward the mansion.

In his talons, he clutched a snake.

"Nkosi," Prescott hissed. "I gotta go."

"There," Caroline stated. "You're tied off." She removed her hands from him, then pointed at him. "But don't you move so fast that you get lightheaded. You lost a lot of blood."

Prescott kept that in mind even as he started toward the central staircase. He rushed up them. Pausing on the second floor, he swayed and blinked, holding tight to the railing.

After a shake of his head, Prescott headed down the hall. He found the door that led to the turret and opened it. Then he climbed the circular stairs to the observation tower.

"Gilbert? Nkosi?" Prescott glanced around, searching for either.

A caw came from the windowsill to his left. He rushed over and found a black mamba curled up on the floor beneath the window. After a second of hesitation, he knelt and slid his fingertips along the animal's lean form.

The blue-black scales were supple and smooth, moving beneath Prescott's fingertips. He carefully stretched out his mate's animal form, searching for issues. While he was no snake expert, he couldn't seem to find any.

Then Prescott spotted the blood marring the left side of Nkosi's head, and he whimpered.

How badly was Nkosi hit in the head?

Prescott gently picked up Nkosi and cradled him to his

chest as he stood. Hurrying down the stairs, he headed toward the second story bedrooms. He peered into each one he passed, searching for one of the medical personnel that had joined them at Shane's estate.

In the third room, Prescott found Darcy, a camel shifter. She and her brother Diamond were both surgeons and had volunteered to help. Even though she was working on a wounded coyote shifter, she paused and looked at him.

"My mate was almost trampled by a rhino," Prescott quickly explained, indicating the snake in his hands. "There's blood on his head." Tears burned the backs of his eyes. "I-I—"

"Help him," the shifter on the bed urged, pain filling his voice. "I'll be fine for a bit."

Darcy scoffed and shook her head. "Only if you want to bleed out." She reached over and hit a button on a device sitting on the nightstand. "Diamond?"

A second later, a deep masculine voice responded, "Yeah, Darc?"

"A possible head trauma to a small shifter just came in," Darcy told him. "You about done there?"

"Yeah," Diamond replied immediately. "Send him to room seven. I'll have Lupine head over there with the X-ray machine."

"Thanks, Dia." Darcy hit the button again, then gave Prescott a reassuring smile. "They'll help your mate."

Prescott turned and hustled down the hallway. He found the indicated room and entered. Standing by the bed, he stared at his mate in his hands, fear and uncertainty filling him.

"Hey, Pres."

Prescott turned and spotted Lupine, a deer shifter. "Hi," he barely managed to squeak out.

Lupine's attention dropped to Nkosi, and he smiled reassuringly. "Lay him on the bed. We'll see what we can do for him. Okay?"

Carefully, Prescott stretched Nkosi out on the bed. The blood appeared to have dried, but he still didn't wake. He bit his bottom lip, fighting to keep in his whimper of pain.

"While you get that machine set up, Lupine, I'll clean him up," Diamond stated, announcing his presence. He paused an instant to squeeze Prescott's shoulder in reassurance. Then Diamond pulled on a pair of gloves before grabbing supplies.

"Yes, Doc," Lupine replied, doing something with the machine he'd wheeled into the room.

"Prescott!"

Prescott turned just in time to catch Hector. His fellow shifter hadn't been allowed in battle—not that he'd wanted to be—but he was at the estate. The scops owl wrapped around Prescott, offering the support and comfort of a flock-mate.

Wrapping his arms around the much smaller man, Prescott sighed and clung to him.

"Don't worry, Pres," Hector murmured, petting his back soothingly. "Your mate will be fine. I can't wait to meet him in human form. I'm not a fan of snakes, but he doesn't seem so bad." Then his dark eyes widened, and a smile curved his lips. "Hey, do you think he knows how to play? If he doesn't, we can teach him." Just as quickly, Hector furrowed his brows. "You don't think he would really bite any of us, do you? I heard he can poison people and make them sleep for a really long time. When they wake up, they feel sick."

Prescott's heartrate slowed as he listened to Hector's prattle. The hyper shifter could always bring a smile to his lips. It did then, too—just a small one.

"I'm sure Nkosi won't bite any of us," Prescott assured Hector. "And I don't know if he knows how to play. We might have to teach him."

"Wait a sec," Lupine cut in. "This is Nkosi? Why the hell are we trying to help one of the rebels?" He glared at Prescott as he crossed his arms over his chest. "We should be dropping him in a cage, not spending our resources on him."

Growling under his breath, Prescott scowled at Lupine. "Nkosi is *not* a rebel. He's helping us." He glanced between the men. Even Diamond had paused, a look of uncertainty on his face. He narrowed his eyes at the doctor. "How do you think we knew about this attack ahead of time?" Prescott pointed at Nkosi. "My mate put his life on the line to help everyone on the council and every other free shifter out there. He's a hero."

Diamond cleared his throat before dipping his chin in a nod. "Okay. I mean, obviously a spy's identity couldn't be shared with the peanut gallery, but it's obvious you believe your words." He smiled and resumed cleaning Nkosi's head. "I'll confirm it with Councilman Alvaro later before allowing Nkosi to wake, but we'll get him squared away in the meantime." Glancing at Lupine, Diamond ordered, "Finish setting that up."

While Lupine appeared mutinous, he started moving again.

Good enough.

CHAPTER EIGHT

Nkosi's head throbbed. Waves of pain pulsed through his temple, robbing him of his focus. He struggled to remember what happened.

After several long, deep breaths, Nkosi realized he was in his black mamba form. If he'd been human, he would have frowned. He didn't traditionally sleep as his snake — hunting and fighting, yes — sleeping, no.

Memories flitted through Nkosi's mind.

The fight.

Him biting several of the shifters and humans with him.

Kennedy realizing Nkosi's betrayal.

The massive rhino attempting to stomp him flat.

Then . . . nothing.

So where am I?

The sound of a door opening drew Nkosi's attention. The thud of it closing again caused a fresh wave of pain through his head. Nkosi reared and hissed, warning whoever away, since he wasn't certain where he was or who with.

"Nkosi? Oh, gods. You're finally awake."

While the voice sounded familiar, Nkosi couldn't place it. He coiled in on himself as he peered intensely in the direction of the speaker, but his vision remained blurry. Hissing again, he struggled to orient himself.

"Nkosi?" The man spoke softer that time. "You're safe, Nkosi. You'll heal."

Nkosi flicked out his tongue, tasting the air around him. The pleasant flavor of his mate exploded across his taste buds.

His snake body shivered at the pleasurable sensation.

Prescott.

My mate is here.

And he said I'd heal. From what?

The image of massive rhino feet coming at him pulsed through his mind once more. He'd attempted to weave between them while searching for a chance to bite Kennedy. Evidently, he hadn't succeeded.

Reaching for his human form, Nkosi began to shift. His body slowly changed, growing larger. The scales on his skin morphed into flesh. Finally, his skull changed shape, retracting his venom glands into a hidden pouch along his nasal cavity.

Nkosi trembled, shudders racking him. He couldn't remember a time when it had hurt so much to shift. Nor could he recall shifting so slowly since youth.

"Hey," Prescott murmured.

Feeling the touch of smooth skin against his hand, Nkosi gripped the other man. He had his eyes open, but he wasn't seeing much. What he assumed was the ceiling overhead was a cloud of gray.

"Hi," Nkosi managed to mutter. His throat felt dry and scratchy, and his head throbbed. He felt sweat on his skin, but it did little to chill the heat flooding him. "Water?"

Let's start simple.

"Of course."

Prescott loosened his hold, as if to move away, and Nkosi tightened his grip. His mate's second hand cradled his. He squeezed rhythmically.

"I'm not going anywhere," Prescott told him reassuringly. "Just over there to the dresser. You'll be able to see me the whole time."

Nkosi turned his head and tried to focus on Prescott. There wasn't much more than a shadow against a lighter background. "Afraid not, Prescott," Nkosi forced himself to admit.

"I can't see much."

"Oh." It sounded as if Prescott said that around a gasp. "I-I'm sorry."

Shaking his head, Nkosi allowed his eyes to close. "Don't apologize for what isn't your fault." He sighed. "Did they get Kennedy?"

"Let me get you the water," Prescott urged after one more squeeze. "And some painkillers."

"Painkillers?" It took every bit of control Nkosi had left to uncurl his fingers. He couldn't remember the last time he'd felt so helpless. "Shifters can't—" Nkosi paused, his dry throat giving out on him.

The sound of Prescott moving around the room told Nkosi of his mate's progress. He turned his head and listened to the trickle of water being poured into a glass. Paper tearing came next.

Prescott's footsteps headed his way. He just managed to keep from jolting when his mate rested one hand on his forearm. Squeezing lightly, Prescott told him, "I'm going to lift your head. Open your mouth for the straw."

Nkosi nodded in acknowledgment. Then Prescott's hand moved. He slid long fingers under Nkosi's head and helped him lift just a little. A straw prodded at his lower lip, and he opened.

Sucking on the straw, Nkosi moaned softly as the cool water flowed across his tongue. He drank and drank, until Prescott pulled the straw away.

"Easy, my mate," Prescott soothed with a squeeze to his neck. "You've been out for a couple of days. I don't want your stomach to get upset."

"Damn," Nkosi grumbled. "Really?"

Prescott might have nodded, but Nkosi couldn't be sure. "The doc said head injuries can be tricky." He pressed something small against his bottom lip. "This is a painkiller designed by a doctor in Stone Ridge for shifters. It'll help."

Knowing his mate came from that town almost two years before, Nkosi trusted him and accepted what felt like a small pill on his tongue. The straw returned, and he drank a bit more. Then Prescott allowed him to relax back on the bed.

"Hopefully, it won't take long to kick in," Prescott murmured.

Nkosi sighed. "Guess I better talk to the doc." Then he drew his brows together. "Baby." He lifted a hand, and Prescott immediately took it. "You didn't answer a couple of my earlier questions."

"Oh." Prescott sounded genuinely surprised, so maybe it hadn't been on purpose. "Which ones?"

Smiling a smidge, Nkosi found he enjoyed the openness of his mate. After spending the last almost two years having to guard everything he said and needing to analyze everything everyone else said, it was refreshing . . . and freeing. Nkosi realized he would never need to guess at Prescott's intentions.

"Where am I?"

"As soon as you were confirmed stable, we moved you to Councilman Goldstein's estate." Prescott sounded nervous as he added, "It's where I live with my flock, so, um . . . I hope you don't mind."

Nkosi squeezed Prescott's hand. "I don't mind. And did Kennedy get caught?"

Prescott cleared his throat. "Sort of. He was attacked by lions, and he's dead now."

Sighing, Nkosi nodded once. "Couldn't have happened to a nicer guy."

"I should let everyone know you woke up," Prescott told him, once more cradling his hand. "I was so damn worried about you."

A hitch sounded in his mate's voice, causing a stab of . . .

something . . . in the vicinity of Nkosi's heart. "Oh, baby," he crooned, lifting his other hand to skim up Prescott's arm. "I—" His fingers ran into a bandage and realization hit. "I am not the only one injured. What happened?"

Prescott's shoulders moved, telling Nkosi he shrugged. "It's nothing. Just a graze."

Nkosi felt as if his heart skipped a beat. "Were you in the battle?"

Gods, please say no. My mate isn't a fighter.

"Not really," Prescott told him.

"What does that mean?" Nkosi asked softly, doing his best not to come across as a demanding asshole.

Prescott rubbed his palm over Nkosi's chest in an obvious attempt to soothe. "You remember those blue lights that flicked on right before the explosions?"

"I do," Nkosi confirmed.

Vincentius had warned him to get away from the lights. When the grenades had been tossed and the explosions began in those areas, he'd been grateful for the councilman's warning. Otherwise, he would have been caught at the fringe of one of the attacks.

"Well, three of us fliers tossed the grenades from nests in the trees, and I was one of them," Prescott explained, sounding proud to do his part. "Then we flew back to the estate. I was injured flying back, but I made it."

Nkosi swallowed his fear upon hearing that. He realized it was a good thing Vincentius hadn't told him about that plan, because he would have been so damn distracted. Even knowing Prescott could be out there flying bandages or ammunition to the snipers had diverted his attention enough. That was never a good thing to be in battle.

After swallowing hard, Nkosi whispered, "I'm glad you're okay, my mate."

Prescott rubbed his palm up Nkosi's chest until he cradled his jaw. "I'll go get a few people."

Feeling Prescott's breath against his lips, Nkosi realized his mate intended to kiss him. He smiled, more than on board with that. When Nkosi felt Prescott's mouth against his own, he gripped his lover's nape.

Nkosi teased his tongue along the seam of Prescott's lips. His mate immediately opened, and he dove inside him. He lapped along his lover's appendage, tasting and mapping anew.

When Prescott's fingers slid along Nkosi's temple, as if aiming for his hair, a shard of pain stabbed through his head. He grunted, turning his head and ending the kiss. His breath rasped as he shuddered.

"Shit," Prescott hissed. "I'm so sorry."

"It's okay, Pres," Nkosi managed to get out between clenched teeth. "We both got carried away."

"I'll get Doctor Diamond," Prescott told him before pecking his forehead.

Nkosi barely registered the opening and closing of the door. Focusing on taking deep even breaths, he slowly regained control of himself. The roaring in his ears subsided, and he relaxed on the bed. In fact, Nkosi's pain began to ebb, too.

Huh. Guess that painkiller is pretty good.

Blinking his eyes open once more, Nkosi peered around the room. He made out hazy shapes and could guess what they were, but he didn't truly see features. Grimacing, he wondered what the hell had happened to fuck up his eyesight.

I'm a shifter. I'll heal.

Nkosi sure hoped he wasn't lying to himself. He forced himself to ease to a sitting position and took the opportunity to skim his palms over the rest of his body. While Nkosi didn't feel pain coming from any other part of himself, he didn't know if the trauma to his head was masking it.

To Nkosi's relief, he found no other bandages or spikes of

pain anywhere. He did, however, feel the sheet at the bottom of the bed and a pillow at the top. Grabbing the sheet, he pulled it over himself to his chest as he settled his head on the pillow.

Feeling around his head slowly, Nkosi discovered where the majority of the pain originated. His left temple had an impressive lump on it. That had to have been where Prescott had inadvertently touched while they'd been kissing.

The sound of the door opening pulled Nkosi away from his mental catalog of his injuries.

Nkosi focused on the blobs entering the room. Several of them separated, standing around the room. He inhaled, using his sense of smell to figure out identities.

While Prescott returned to his side and took his hand, Nkosi greeted Vincentius. "Councilman Goldstein, thank you for the care in your home."

"You're welcome, Nkosi," Vincentius replied, the sound coming from the large figure to his left. "It's good to see you awake once more."

"I'm Doctor Diamond Sucrose," the male approaching the right side of the bed told him—a quick sniff told Nkosi that the guy was a camel shifter. "Prescott mentioned some complications."

Nkosi squeezed Prescott's hand even as he arched one brow. "I suppose one could call vision problems a complication."

Diamond sighed so softly that Nkosi almost missed it. "I apologize for making light of your condition, Nkosi," he stated. Then he quickly asked, "May I call you Nkosi? Or would you prefer I address you as Mister Akintola?"

Trying to put the uncertain shifter at ease, Nkosi told him, "Nkosi is fine, Doctor." As the scent of relief teased his nostrils, he asked, "Any idea why I can't see much more than blobs?"

"I'm not an eye specialist," Diamond admitted even as he shown a penlight into Nkosi's left eye. "Please stare straight ahead."

Nkosi did as he was told. A moment later, the light moved to his other eye.

After Diamond flicked off the light, he must have put it somewhere. His fingers felt around his skull. When he hit the swollen patch, Nkosi hissed.

"There's still a lot of swelling through here, even with your increased healing." Diamond sounded concerned. "Also because you're a shifter, I can't send you to an eye specialist. I don't know of any."

"I'll ask around," Vincentius cut in. "See if any other doctors know of a paranormal eye specialist."

Nkosi nodded once. "Thanks."

"Is there nothing you can do?" Prescott asked tentatively.

Diamond hummed. "I can borrow some equipment and take pictures of his eyes. I'll give them to a human specialist and let him know the patient is out of town, so he can't be seen in person." It sounded as if Diamond was rubbing the back of his neck. "It's also possible that as your swelling goes down, your eyesight will return."

Nodding once, Nkosi did his best to put on a brave face. "Anything is possible with shifter healing."

"Exactly," Diamond confirmed, sounding a bit more confident. "I'll arrange to borrow the equipment and be back in a day or two. In the meantime, how's your pain level? Prescott said he gave you the medication."

Nkosi squeezed Prescott's hand, casting a smile in his direction. "He did, and I feel . . . pretty good." Arching a brow, he added, "I don't feel that druggy haze I've heard humans talk about when on strong meds, and my head only aches a little."

"I'm glad to hear it." Diamond sounded and scented sincere. He patted Nkosi's shoulder. "We'll figure this out. You're a hero." Then the doctor turned and left the room.

Scoffing softly, Nkosi rolled his eyes. "I'm no hero."

"Yes, you are," Vincentius countered, his deep voice filled with certainty. "Due to your sacrifice, your intel and tenacity, we were not only able to defend Shane's home, but clear out all the warehouses, too." A hard edge filled his tone. "Kontra's people and Raven teamed up with the Drudeson brothers and a few other council enforcers. They captured Paraben, and now all his files are in Jared and Raven's hands. Between that and you telling us the names of his scientist and military contacts, I bet we'll be able to learn where hundreds of missing shifters ended up."

"I certainly hope so," Nkosi stated, relief filling him that if he had sacrificed his vision, it wasn't in vain.

That's something, right?

"I'm going to order some food for you," Vincentius told him, patting his foot. "For you and Prescott."

"Councilman?" Nkosi called as he saw the lion shifter's blob move toward the door. "Are all the rebels accounted for?"

Vincentius hesitated, then told him, "Everyone but two. The tiger shifter Mindy, and a buffalo shifter named Warsaw."

Nkosi's brows shot up. "Uh, I know where Warsaw is."

"Really?" Vincentius moved back toward him. "Where?"

Grimacing, Nkosi admitted, "My house. I told him I'd get him when the fighting was over."

Prescott growled, surprising him. "Why do you have another shifter in your home?"

Nkosi smiled at his mate, surprisingly pleased that his mate felt jealous of another on his behalf.

Now he knows how I felt when we met.

"Down, my mate," Nkosi teased with a wink. "I was help-ing Warsaw defect. He joined because he was best friends with Kennedy, and he says he's regretted it ever since." Shrugging, Nkosi added, "As soon as I'm well enough, I'll take you to my place to collect him. He knows he'll be in trou-ble, but he refused to help the rogues anymore."

"So, one then. Mindy."

Groaning, Nkosi muttered, "She'll be tough to pin down. She's a squirrely, manipulative bitch."

Vincentius hummed. "Good to know. See you soon."

Nkosi heard the door close, then felt Prescott ease onto the bed beside him. That wasn't close enough. He wrapped his arm around his mate and tugged.

"Get up here, Prescott," Nkosi ordered, squeezing his hip. "I want to hold you."

Prescott didn't need to be asked twice.

Relaxing with his mate in his arms for the first time — ever — Nkosi felt a bout of nerves break over him.

"What's the matter?" Prescott had obviously scented it.

Nkosi realized if he couldn't share with his mate, he had no business holding him. He turned his head and stared at the figure in his arms. "What if I never regain my sight?"

CHAPTER NINE

You're my mate. I'll take you any way I can get you.

Prescott walked beside Nkosi as they moved slowly down the hall, remembering the words he'd told his mate the previous day. In his memory, it sounded like a platitude. He just hadn't known what else to say.

Plus, it was exactly how he felt. He'd never cared what kind of package his mate came in. Regardless of his diminished eyesight, Nkosi was still the most amazing man he'd ever known, and he wanted him.

And once he's healthy again, I'm gonna have him. Or have him have me.

Smiling at the thought, Prescott continued to guide Nkosi through their new home. They were going to join the others for breakfast, first. After that, Nkosi would take them to his home to collect Warsaw.

Nkosi had given Cho access to a camera in his home the prior evening, so they'd been able to confirm that a very nervous Warsaw was still residing there.

"What has you so happy?"

Upon hearing Nkosi's question, Prescott focused on him. "How do you know I'm smiling?" he teased, grinning even wider.

A small smile teased at the corners of Nkosi's lips as he tilted his head. "Your scent, my mate," he purred. Leaning closer, he nuzzled his nose into Prescott's chest. "You smell happy."

"Yeah, I'm happy," Prescott admitted, squeezing Nkosi's

hand, which was resting in the crook of his elbow. "Just being with you makes me happy." Chuckling, he added, "Plus, I was thinking about when you feel better, when you're not plagued by unexpected headaches." Prescott dipped his head and growled into Nkosi's ear, "I'm gonna love on you so good, my mate. You're mine."

Nkosi hummed as he smiled faintly. "You sure you don't want to wait until we know about my eyesight?" He had his left hand in the crook of Prescott's arm, and he skimmed the fingertips of his other along the wall. "I may never be better, like you think."

Growling under his breath, Prescott turned. He gripped Nkosi's jaw and used the hold to tip his head up. "Nkosi, if I were a blind human, would you not want me?"

A stricken look crossed Nkosi's face. "No, of course, I would."

"Why do you think this is different?" Prescott needed to understand his mate.

Nkosi sighed deeply, his murky-black eyes closing. "I've been a self-sufficient enforcer for almost two centuries, Prescott," he told him quietly. "The idea of having to rely on someone else for basic needs, even my mate"—a muscle ticked in his jaw before he admitted—"it bothers me."

"Basic needs," Prescott repeated slowly. "Do you mean like getting from point A to point B?"

Scoffing, Nkosi nodded. "Yes. Getting from the bedroom to the dining room."

"Blind people learn their homes and get around just fine." Prescott pecked a kiss to Nkosi's lips. "You'll learn." Then he turned them back in the direction of the dining room.

"I won't be able to drive, though," Nkosi grumbled. "What about my bike?"

Prescott shook his head. "I can't drive. When you drove me home, did it make me less?"

Nkosi groaned as he tipped his head back. "Gods, I'm being a whiny brat, aren't I?" Huffing a sigh, he muttered, "I'm sorry, baby."

"No need to apologize. This is new," Prescott pointed out. "Besides, we still don't even know if it's permanent. It's only been a day."

"And if it *is* permanent, Prescott," Nkosi asked persistently.

Growling, Prescott grumbled, "I thought I already told you. I'll take you any way I can get you." Then a thought struck, and his heartrate spiked in his chest. "If it does end up permanent, would you prefer to have died? To have left me?" Prescott swallowed hard before finishing in a small voice he couldn't seem to control, "If you don't have your eyesight, life with me isn't worth living?"

"Oh, fuck," Nkosi snarled, tightening his hold on Prescott's arm. He swung him around to face him. His right hand fumbled a little before he used it to grip Prescott's upper arm. "Get that thought out of your head right now, baby," Nkosi demanded. "That's not what I'm saying at all."

"It sounded like it," Prescott whispered, staring into Nkosi's dark features, trying to read the feral expression there.

Nkosi shook his head. "That's *not* what I said. That's *not* what I meant." Even without being able to see clearly, he still pinned him with a feral stare. "I see I'm already fucking up this relationship of ours, and we've barely gotten started." Tightening his right hand on Prescott's elbow, Nkosi wound his right around his waist and tugged him close, flushing their bodies. "You are mine, Prescott. I will always want you. Yes, I'm freaking out about my eyes, but that has nothing to do with you and how much I want you."

Reading the intensity in Nkosi's features and scenting his

sincerity, Prescott nodded. "Okay," he murmured upon remembering his mate couldn't see the move.

That will take some getting used to.

"I suppose we both have some adjustments to make, Prescott," Nkosi told him. "Just because we're both shifters doesn't mean our relationship will click in all easy." His smile appeared wry as he told him, "Relationships take work. We're complete strangers that come from different backgrounds. It'll take some time to figure each other out."

Prescott nodded, then mentally kicked himself once more. "You're right, of course." A chuckle escaped him as he thought about what his flock-mates had gone through while working things out with their mates. Another idea poked him, and he couldn't help but grin. "Was this our first fight?" Upon seeing Nkosi's left eyebrow arch in silent question, Prescott snickered as he dipped his head so he could whisper into his ear, "I've been told make-up sex is awesome."

Nkosi chuckled, and the sound warmed Prescott like nothing else ever could. Finally, his mate was beginning to relax. Just like any shifter, Prescott wanted his love happy.

Hopefully healthy will come soon, too.

"We'll discuss make-up sex soon enough, Prescott," Nkosi rumbled, sliding his hand down to cup his ass. He gave it a squeeze. "Very, very soon."

A zing of arousal burst through his veins, and he rocked his hips on a moan. His prick began to thicken, and his breathing picked up. He rubbed his own palms up and down Nkosi's back, exploring the lean muscle beneath the polo shirt he wore.

Just as Prescott lowered his head, intending to kiss his mate, a gruff voice muttered, "Before ya fuck him right in the hall, will you let us pass, Prescott? I'm hungry."

Prescott straightened, turning his head to glare at Thad.

"Oh, hon," Lachlan murmured from where he stood next to Thad, his arm around his waist. "You're such a cockblocker."

Thad shrugged one shoulder. "I'm hungry."

Lachlan rumbled huskily as he quipped back, "That's because we already worked up an appetite."

While Prescott groaned, Nkosi snorted. He allowed his mate to turn him, loosening his hold. "Come on." As if on cue, Nkosi's stomach rumbled. "I'm hungry, too."

Prescott conceded defeat and began leading Nkosi down the hallway again. "You did only have soup yesterday."

"Which sort of sucked," Nkosi stated. "I like meat."

"Doctor's orders," Lachlan commented from behind them. He patted Nkosi on the shoulder. "And we're glad to have you back, my friend."

For a second, Prescott fought the urge to growl at the cat shifter. A squeeze to his arm and Nkosi urging him to relax settled him. He shook his head, surprised at his possessive reaction.

"You and your animal will settle a bit once you've completed your mating," Lachlan stated, not sounding at all upset. "I worked with Nkosi for over a century, and don't worry." His tone held amusement. "There's never been anything but friendship between us. Not my type."

"Nor are you mine," Nkosi responded dryly, a smirk curving his lips.

Lachlan just laughed.

"The end of the hall is coming up," Prescott told Nkosi, shifting gears. "There's a door that leads into the formal dining room, but we only use it if there's a huge group. Otherwise, we eat in the small dining room." He squeezed his mate's hand, then urged him to turn. "Feel the door frame in front of you."

Nkosi did as instructed while narrowing his eyes.

Perhaps he doesn't like an audience.

As much as Prescott didn't want to have another conversation with Nkosi about learning to do things while blind, he feared it would be in their future.

Damn.

Prescott realized Nkosi was searching for a door handle and grimaced. "I'm sorry, this is a swinging door. It leads into a large laundry space, so they probably made it that way so people carrying laundry don't have to fight with a knob."

Murmuring *ahh*, Nkosi pushed. "Since the bedrooms are to the left, I presume there will be another door somewhere to the right?"

"Yes. Ten feet forward and eight to the right." Prescott did his best to explain the dimensions. "But there's a counter on the right, too, so be careful."

Nkosi reached out and felt for the counter, finding it on the second try. "Another swinging door? Or a knob?"

Prescott allowed Nkosi to explore, keeping pace with him. He appreciated that Thad and Lachlan remained silent . . . and patient. Prescott had no idea how the dominant male would react to them skirting around him to pass.

"Another push door," Prescott told Nkosi as they rounded the counter. "Then, the dining room table will be eight feet in front of you. Uh, chairs before it."

Nodding, Nkosi pushed the door open and walked slowly into the room, his hand stretched out before him. The sound of cutlery hitting dishes and the chatter of voices ceased. For a second, Nkosi paused before starting forward again.

"Welcome, Nkosi," Seever greeted from the other side of the table. "Good to see you on your feet."

"Thank you," Nkosi replied with a small smile. "Good to be on my feet."

Lachlan and Thad moved behind them to the right, rounding the table. "Do you still not drink coffee?" Lachlan asked.

Nkosi touched a chair in front of him and curled his fingers around the cloth back. "Correct."

"What kind of tea?" Thad asked. "We fliers aren't much for coffee, either, so there's plenty of tea flavors available." His voice turned gruff as he added, "Bein' in a cage, never acquired a taste for it after we got out."

Feeling around the chair, Nkosi let go of Prescott. "Anything black is fine." As he rounded the furniture and settled in it, he added, "No honey or sugar. I get enough of that off the pastries I love."

Prescott rested his hand on Nkosi's shoulder as he leaned over him. Nuzzling his mate's neck, he murmured, "What's your favorite pasty? There's normally a variety of donuts, muffins, and cinnamon rolls."

Nkosi turned his head and pressed a kiss to Prescott's cheek. "Are the cinnamon rolls covered in icing?"

Smiling, Prescott turned his own head and slid his lips along his mate's in a barely-there kiss. "Is there any other way to eat a cinnamon roll?"

Chuckling, Nkosi quipped, "Some people are sacrilegious that way."

Prescott licked Nkosi's lower lip before whispering, "I'll get you one." As he straightened, he asked, "What's your protein preference? Eggs? Bacon? Sausage?"

"Any or all of the above would be fantastic," Nkosi replied. Then he shook his head. "Maybe not the eggs. Not sure I'm up to a fork, yet."

Realizing what Nkosi meant, Prescott told him, "You got it." At least he was loosening up.

Prescott passed Thad, who was carrying an extra cup of English Breakfast tea. He smiled in thanks to his flock-mate. Thad nodded back.

Reaching the bar area that opened to the kitchen on the other side, Prescott spotted Reese in there at the stove. "Morning, Reese." As he looked over the selections, he hummed. "Everything looks and smells fantastic."

"Morning." Reese peered over his shoulder and grinned. "Oh, it'll taste fantastic, too."

"It always does," Prescott responded with a grin.

Then Prescott began filling up two plates. He placed a cinnamon roll dripping with icing on one plate. To that one, he added four slices of bacon, four sausage links, and a scoop of fruit salad. Prescott hoped his lover didn't mind picking up the fruit with his fingers.

After adding the same to his own plate — minus the cinnamon roll — Prescott also scooped up some cheesy scrambled eggs and hash browns. He hefted both plates and returned to the table. To his surprise, he found a cup of tea in front of his own setting, as well as a roll of silverware.

Glancing around the table, Prescott saw Ashton wink. He hadn't even realized his alpha had entered. Ranger was engaging Nkosi in conversation, and from the sounds of it, they were swapping stories about their times working with Paraben.

It didn't sound like fun.

Prescott set the plates in front of their respective places, then pulled his chair out. He didn't know if it was the sound of the chair, his own scent, or the smell of the food, but Nkosi paused in his conversation.

"Thank you, baby," Nkosi murmured. "It all smells amazing."

"Reese always assures me that it will taste amazing, too," Prescott told him with a soft chuckle. Squeezing Nkosi's thigh, he told him what was on his plate. "I also added a scoop of fruit salad. They're big chunks, so easy to pick up."

Nkosi nodded. "Thank you again." By feel, he snagged a strip of bacon and began to eat.

The conversation resumed around them, and to Prescott, it felt like every other morning with his flock.

Except better, because now I have my mate by my side.

CHAPTER TEN

Riding in a car when unable to see much caused a hint of nausea to churn in Nkosi's gut.

Huh. That's so not a good thing.

Nkosi shifted in his seat uncomfortably. When that didn't help, he swallowed convulsively. His mouth became dry, and he couldn't get enough moisture in his throat.

"Hey. Hey," Prescott murmured into his ear, pulling him flush to his side with a strong arm around his waist. "Drink. It's water."

An open bottle touched Nkosi's bottom lip, and he gripped it. Tipping his head back, he took a large sip. He let it roll over his tongue for a few seconds before swallowing it.

For the next several minutes, that was all Nkosi focused on.

"Feeling better?" Prescott asked, touching his lips to the lobe of Nkosi's ear. "Stomach settling?"

"How'd you know?" Nkosi answered, since he didn't want to admit that his gut still churned.

Prescott nuzzled his nose into the crook of Nkosi's neck as he whispered, "With the amount of times I've been stuck in animal form, in a cage, with a bunch of my flock-mates, in the back of a swaying truck, I recognized the signs. Just because you're in human form didn't lessen the tightness of your features or the way you swallowed." After nipping Nkosi's neck, he added softly, "And you didn't answer my question."

Nkosi groaned quietly as he admitted, "You're right. Never considered riding in a car without my sight would cause an issue."

"Tuck your nose into your mate's neck and take in his scent." Enforcer Dakota Drudeson's deep voice sounded from in front of him. "It's supposed to be soothing."

Nkosi had heard that Dakota—a komodo dragon shifter and the youngest of the three Drudeson brothers—was driving.

"It *is* soothing." That was Enforcer Tideus Solverman, a saltwater crocodile. "Jin's scent always calms me after a rough day."

Tideus had recently mated with a human restaurant owner and had been sickenly happy ever since. Well, that was what Nkosi had heard, since he hadn't been around. He looked forward to reconnecting with the other enforcers.

Taking the pair's advice, Nkosi turned his head and burrowed into Prescott's side. He felt how his mate slouched a little in his seat. His duck shifter tucked him close and hummed appreciatively as he arched his neck back, giving him plenty of room.

Nkosi would never have thought he would end up in such a position . . . the one getting comfort from his mate. While he wasn't a large man—probably even considered small for a shifter—his snake was dominant. Still, as Prescott's woodsy, masculine scent filled his nostrils, he couldn't deny the satisfaction he felt.

Even his snake curled up and relaxed in his mind.

I'm safe with my mate.

That thought brought another to Nkosi's mind.

I want to claim my mate.

Nkosi's body heated as he reveled in Prescott's delicious aroma. His blood flowed to his prick, and he began to thicken in his jeans. He flicked out his tongue and swiped the sweat from Prescott's skin.

Growling softly, Nkosi began to suckle on the warm flesh beneath his lips.

Prescott moaned softly, the sound vibrating through

Nkosi. When he felt his mate cup his head and squeeze encouragingly, he sucked harder. Nkosi relished the heady scent of Prescott's arousal, the smell flooding his senses.

"Aaaaand, ladies and gentlemen. It looks like we're going to get a show this evening."

Delanrue Drudeson's voice came from behind Nkosi. He was the oldest of the three siblings. While his rank was Council Enforcer, he was also an interrogation expert. Nkosi hadn't been certain why Delanrue had been ordered to attend the take in.

Then what Delanrue had actually said registered in Nkosi's brain. He lifted his head and focused an angry glare toward the rear of the large SUV. While he couldn't make out much more than the shape of someone in the backseat behind him, Nkosi still snarled the man's name.

Letting out a low, husky chuckle, Delanrue rumbled, "What's wrong, Nkosi?" There was a definite hint of a smirk in his tone. "Don't like someone recording while you make out?"

Prescott growled as he tightened his hold on Nkosi. "What the hell's your problem, dude?" Then his voice took on a sultry tone as he mused, "Oh, I see. You haven't gotten laid in a while, and you need something for your spank bank." Even while Nkosi heard Delanrue's warning growl, Prescott let out a put-upon sigh. "I know we're hot together, but you'll have to buy your porn just like everyone else."

"Why you little—" Delanrue began, a definite snarl in his voice.

To Nkosi's relief, Dakota barked, "Delanrue, knock it off. You know we started it."

Even as Delanrue continued to growl, Tideus added, "I'm sorry, guys. I'm the one who made the *record them* gesture to Del." He heaved a sigh. "You're not mated, yet, so of course you'd overreact. Sorry, guys."

Delanrue heaved an annoyed sigh. "Fine. You get a pass."

Prescott snorted. "Oh, how big of you."

"Let it go, Pres," Nkosi urged, squeezing his thigh.

"Very well," Prescott muttered. "He's probably just jealous, anyway."

"I know I am," Dakota piped up from the front. "Hot little number like you. Mmm-mmm."

It was Nkosi's turn to growl.

"Man, you guys are horrible," Tideus said on a laugh.

After a soft grumble under his breath, Delanrue admitted, "Yeah, I want my mate, too. Not that either of you are my type."

"What is your type?" Prescott asked curiously. While he continued to keep one arm around Nkosi, from the feel of it, he'd half turned around in the seat. "Male? Female? Human? Shifter? Vampire?" His tone brightened. "I know soooo many people."

For a few seconds, silence reined in the SUV.

Finally, Delanrue cleared his throat in obvious discomfort. "I don't care about any of that as long as they're big," he mumbled, sounding as uncomfortable as hell. "I don't wanna have to censor my strength too much."

Nkosi never would have thought he would see the day. Baddass interrogator Delanrue Drudeson was embarrassed. Even his scent gave him away.

Go figure.

"Someone big . . ." Prescott mused out loud.

Delanrue must have thought it was a question, for he grunted in confirmation.

Then Prescott gasped and grabbed Nkosi's arm tighter. "Hey, you remember Baden? He's big."

It took every ounce of self-control not to roll his eyes. "Baden from the club?" Nkosi figured they didn't have any other Badens in common, but he double-checked anyway.

"Yeah! We could introduce them." Then Prescott seemed

to deflate beside him. "Oh, but Baden isn't in the market for a relationship. Hmmm."

"Uh, you know that Fate brings our mates to us in a time of need, right?" Tideus pointed out. "Set-ups don't normally work."

Prescott hummed. "Well, *all* my flock-mates have found their mates, so now we need to help you all." He sounded so matter of fact as he added, "Besides, Tideus. You didn't find your mate until *we* were in the area. Stick with us, boys. My flock is good luck."

Dakota chuckled softly. "Okay, cutie. We'll stick with you all. Right, bro?"

That earned another low grunt from the eldest brother.

"We're here," Tideus proclaimed. "Oh, damn. You really live here?"

Nkosi knew what his place looked like—a small, neat cottage with a garden full of flowers. It really did appear like something out of a picture book. Flower gardening was Nkosi's guilty secret, but he guessed that cat was out of the bag now.

Not sure if I'll be able to enjoy it much anymore now, anyway.

Banishing that thought, Nkosi listened as the engine stopped. He heard doors opening and closing. Then Prescott gripped his hand.

"Come on," Prescott encouraged. "You know your walk to your front door. You can do this."

"Someone's watching from the window," Tideus warned.

Delanrue sighed. "I'm jogging around back."

"Don't step on my flowers," Nkosi couldn't help but snap as he eased out of the vehicle. The dark splotches were instantly replaced by lighter shadows. Unable to help himself, Nkosi muttered, "Gods, this sucks."

"It'll get better," Prescott purred into his ear as he wrapped Nkosi's hand around his elbow. "Even if better means learning to navigate your surroundings in a different way."

Sighing, Nkosi nodded. "I know, baby. It's just . . . still so new."

Prescott pressed his forehead to Nkosi's temple even as he started them walking. "Believe it or not, I do understand. When we were finally rescued, most of us had to learn *everything*." Softly sighing, he muttered, "And I still can't drive a car, so it's good that I live with people who can do that for me. I'm dependent on them, and it's something I have to live with."

Nkosi murmured, "I know it makes me an asshole, but I wish it was me you were dependent on."

"I know." Prescott pecked a kiss to his cheek.

Then Prescott urged Nkosi to walk a little faster. "Dakota and Tideus got a little ahead of us." Then his breath caught. "Oh, and your front door is opening. We're looking at a big blond. Is that Warsaw?"

"Nkosi?"

Hearing Warsaw's deep voice, Nkosi nodded. "That's him." Louder, he called, "Hey, Warsaw. Sorry it took me so long. I was injured."

Still am, but whatever.

"Okay." Warsaw cleared his throat. "These the enforcers meant to take me in then, huh?"

"Yeah, man," Nkosi confirmed. "But I explained. You'll get a fair shake. Probably have a fair bit of community service and shit to do, though."

Warsaw cleared his throat. "Better than the alternative."

Oh damn.

Nkosi cocked his head. "You talking about Kennedy?"

"Uh, Kennedy?" Warsaw let out a groan. "Ah, he's dead, isn't he?"

"He is," Nkosi confirmed. Then it hit him. "You mean me, because I'm blind?"

"Fuck," Warsaw exclaimed. "You're blind? How the hell did that happen?"

Nkosi rolled his eyes as he shook his head. "Your asshole friend didn't like me helping the other side." He listened to Warsaw groan. Once he was done, he asked, "So what the hell are *you* talking about?"

A low growl entered Warsaw's voice as he stated, "Watching that asshole sell our own kind to scientists. I mean, what the fuck is up with that?" Then he sighed. "And hiding in the closet. Geez, that shit sucks. The amount of bitching my best friend did when he heard about councilmembers being gay or bi or even friendly to it kept me so far deep." Warsaw groaned, the sound one of emotional pain. "Then I fucked up and did this."

"At least now you can make amends," Nkosi stated diplomatically.

Nkosi wasn't certain what else to say. As a snake shifter, he'd rarely had close friends. Peer pressure and wanting to please a buddy to the point of stupidity wasn't really a thing for him.

Cocking his head, thinking of Prescott's mention of setting the enforcers up, Nkosi suddenly wondered if that wouldn't change.

A bridge to cross later . . . how to rein in my mate.

"Thank you for coming along quietly, Warsaw," Dakota stated. "Nkosi said you would, but you understand why we had to take precautions."

"Delanrue," Tideus called. "We got him."

Good thing I don't have nearby neighbors, or they would have been putting on a show.

"Okay. Back to the SUV, I guess," Prescott told him, turning him.

"Wait, uh . . ." Warsaw sounded uncertain.

"Spit it out, man," Dakota told him.

Warsaw cleared his throat. He was close enough to Nkosi for him to scent. Smelling something on the male's clothes, he groaned.

"Did you seriously bring a dog into my home?" Nkosi growled, annoyance flooding him.

With a whine in his voice, Warsaw grumbled, "You didn't come back after the first day, so I had to go get her. I couldn't leave her alone."

"Oh, isn't he cute," Prescott gushed, suddenly leaving Nkosi alone. "Oh, you gotta feel this soft fur. What kind is he?"

"It's a she," Warsaw corrected quietly. "And she's a shih tzu. Her name's Jasmine."

"Aww." Prescott sounded enraptured. "Hello, Jasmine. Who's a pretty girl?" His voice took on a baby-like quality. "Hmm? Is that you?" A second later, Prescott sounded normal when he asked, "Is she good with little kids?"

Warsaw chuckled, sounding relieved. "Yeah, she is." He cleared his throat. "So, uh, you'll care for her while I can't?"

Prescott sounded so damn happy that Nkosi just couldn't counter his mate when he said, "Of course."

"Um, who are you?" Warsaw asked suddenly.

Nkosi snorted as he held out his hand. "This is Prescott." He closed his fingers around his mate's when the duck shifter came to him. "He's my mate."

"Wow," Warsaw muttered, sounding shocked. "When you said you had a mate, never thought it'd be a sensual pretty boy like that."

Growling softly, Nkosi ordered, "Stop looking at my mate."

"Uh, then Prescott really shouldn't dress like that," Dakota muttered with a snicker kicking up the end. "He's hot."

Nkosi focused on Prescott, but all he could do was scent him . . . and his mate smelled a little embarrassed. "Baby, what are you wearing?"

"Nothing I don't wear every day around the estate," Prescott told him. "Jeans, boots, and a polo shirt."

That doesn't sound so bad.

To Nkosi's surprise, Delanrue spoke up as he stalked by, obviously heading back to the SUV. "He's in a pale-green pair of skinny jeans tucked into black platform boots. His light-brown hair is styled in a messy bed-head look, and his light-blue, form-fitting polo shirt brings out his eyes, as does the pale blue eyeliner he's wearing."

Nkosi whipped his focus back to his mate. "You wear club attire around the estate?" He'd noticed that Prescott had been taller than him than when they were barefoot, but he'd figured that was due to their differing choice of footwear.

And obviously, it is.

Huffing a sigh, Prescott pulled away from Nkosi. "It's not club clothes," he countered. "There's no reason not to want to look good, especially when you're going out with your mate."

"Baby." Nkosi held out his hand again, and he waited patiently until his handsome wood duck shifter once again twined their fingers with his own. "Baby," he began again. "I can't see you, so looking good for me is sort of lost on me."

Prescott's tone turned scandalized. "That doesn't mean I want to embarrass you." A whine entered his voice. "Hon, I don't want to just look good *to* you. I want to look good *for* you."

Understanding dawned, and Nkosi nodded. "I see." Then he winked and added, "You know what I mean." Tugging his lover close, Nkosi wrapped his arm around Prescott. "Do you want to know what I really appreciate?"

Nkosi used the feel of the familiar cement walkway to guide his steps.

"What?"

While Nkosi scented the dog, he ignored it. Instead, he rubbed his free hand up and down the silky-soft polo shirt covering his torso.

"It's the fact that you feel and smell so damn good."

Prescott whimpered softly under his touch. "D-Does that mean you're going to claim me when we get home?"

"Sure does." Nkosi refused to leave his mate wanting for a moment longer than necessary. "As soon as we get home, you're mine."

"We're sitting in the back seat so we can make out," Prescott called, earning laughs from the others, even Delanrue and Warsaw.

Chapter Eleven

"You brought a dog?" Seever commented, meeting them in the foyer. He pinned a narrow-eyed gaze on Nkosi, which was totally lost on his blind mate. "I didn't know you had a dog, Nkosi."

Nkosi shook his head. "I don't. This is Warsaw's." Then he grinned. Even with murky-black eyes, they still seemed to sparkle with mischief. "Prescott said he'd take care of him while Warsaw figures his shit out." Winking, Nkosi added, "You know how we like to make our mates happy."

Seever groaned. "But it's a little yip, yip dog. What if it's afraid of our animals?"

"Oh, we'll get her used to them," Prescott countered with a grin. Then he held it out. "But Nkosi is going to claim me now, so do you mind taking care of her?"

Taking a step backward, Seever stared aghast at the cute little animal. Her long, brown and white hair was held back from her eyes by pretty pink bow clips. She panted softly, her little tongue curling. Peering around the massive foyer with curious brown eyes, she wagged her lump of a tail in excitement.

Before Prescott could come up with a way to convince Seever to take the animal — *gods, my dick hurts so bad* — Hector came bouncing down the stairs.

Perfect.

"Hey, Hec," Prescott greeted with a grin. "Look what I got."

Hector froze, staring at the animal in Prescott's arms. For

an instant, he was worried his plan had backfired. Then, predictably, Hector squealed and hopped down the remaining few stairs.

"She's so cute! What is she? Is she potty trained? Does she like kids? Does she do any tricks?"

As usual, the scops owl shifter was off and running with questions.

Prescott grinned broadly . . . until he saw Rocky's face. The man frowned at him, his expression telling him that the human knew exactly what he was trying to pull.

Uh oh. Don't wanna cause problems between mates.

Refocusing on Hector, Prescott gripped his buddy's upper arm with his free hand, gaining his attention from where he petted the dog, which was happily licking a giggling Hector's face.

"This is Jasmine," Prescott told his friend. "She's on loan for a little while because her owner is in custody with the enforcers." Seeing Hector freeze, his expression turning stricken, Prescott hurriedly assured, "He made a bad decision, so he's gonna need to do penance. I was hoping you could help me care for Jasmine while he does." Shifting his focus between Seever and Rocky, Prescott claimed, "She's totally potty trained and is supposed to be great with kids."

At that moment, Jayden, Rocky's son, who'd been sleeping in his arms, roused enough to notice what was going on. His expression brightened, and he made grabby hands in Jasmine's direction. "Puppy!" Jayden cried. "Daddy, Daddy, puppy!"

"Yes, that does look like a puppy, doesn't it, Jayden," Rocky replied, slowly closing the gap between them. He still didn't look impressed with the situation, and Prescott figured he would have some making up to do.

I just wanna get claimed! Is that too much to ask?

Hess's booming laughter filled the foyer. "Damn, Pres. Where did you get this little beauty?"

Oh, thank god. An animal lover.

As Prescott passed over the animal to Hess, he explained about Warsaw and Jasmine.

"Aww . . . did Daddy do something silly, sweetie?" Hess crooned to the animal, which responded by licking his nose. Laughing, Hess grinned at Hector and Rocky. "Come on, guys. Let's get this pretty little girl some water." Then Hess waggled his eyebrows as he tapped his nose with the forefinger of his other hand. "These guys obviously need to get laid."

Prescott groaned. "Yesss," he hissed. "Thank you so much."

Then Prescott grabbed Nkosi, wrapping an arm around his waist. He led them out of the foyer and deeper into the house toward the bedroom suites. Taking a chance, he glanced over his shoulder before the others disappeared from view.

Spotting Hess's waggling brows, Prescott grinned. His mirth and pleasure eased when he spotted Seever's scowl and Rocky's exasperated look. Then the huge, black bodybuilder smirked at Prescott and winked.

Relief flooded Prescott.

We're okay.

"In a hurry, baby?" Nkosi teased once they were striding down the hallway.

"Oh gods, yessss," Prescott replied, answering honestly. "I need your dick in my ass so badly."

Nkosi growled deeply. "Need my seed filling your chute? Need my teeth in your neck?"

To Prescott's surprise, Nkosi spun him and pressed him face-first into the wall. His mate held him in place with his strong, lithe body. He rocked his hips as he skimmed his hands up until he gripped Prescott's wrists, holding them over his head.

"Need me to hold you down and pummel your ass, Pres?" Nkosi growled into his ear. "That's what you need, isn't it?"

"Yessss," Prescott whined. He bucked his hips backward,

pleased to feel his mate's erection grinding against his ass. "Need you, mate. Need."

Nkosi rubbed his jeans-covered dick against Prescott once, twice, more before pulling away. "Get us to your bedroom, Pres, before I take you in this hall just as Thad accused us of this morning."

Right. This morning.

That sobered his ardor just a smidge.

Prescott breathed deeply, trying to get himself under control. The long make-out session suddenly didn't seem like it had been such a good idea. He was supposed to be giving his mate time to heal.

"Hey," Nkosi crooned before suckling his lobe gently. "What just happened? Where did you go?"

"I'm supposed to be giving you time to get rid of your headaches," Prescott pointed out, looking over his shoulder at his mate. "Are you sure you're well enough for this?"

Nkosi's smile appeared a mixture of sultry and sweetness. "Oh, baby. Of course, I'll be fine." Raking his palm slowly over Prescott's chest, he purred, "While it might not be the hard pounding we had in that club bathroom, I'll still make certain you enjoy every second of it."

Then Nkosi's hand landed on Prescott's fly. His mate squeezed and massaged him through the denim of his jeans. He bucked his hips and shuddered, feeling pre-cum ooze from his dick.

"Th-That's not what I-I was w-worried about," Prescott managed to gasp out.

"No?" Nkosi eased his ministrations, although he didn't release him completely. "Then what?"

Prescott let out a long breath before admitting, "I don't want to hurt you or set back your condition."

Nkosi rubbed his cheek against the back of Prescott's neck. "I'm fine. I'll be careful, baby." After nipping his nape, he eased away. "Take me to your room."

"*Our* room," Prescott countered, slowly turning around.

Waiting, he peered into Nkosi's face, trying to read his response to that.

A slow, sensual smile curved Nkosi's full lips. "*Our* room." Grinning, he told him, "We'll pack my place eventually." Then Nkosi waggled his brows. "You gonna help me start a garden here?" Nkosi's playfulness slipped from his features just as quickly. "If I get my sight back."

Prescott turned and wrapped his arm around Nkosi. "Tell you what," he began as he started them moving again. "Even if you don't get your sight back, we'll still create a garden together. It'll just be a lot slower."

Sighing, Nkosi smiled up at Prescott. "Thank you."

Dipping his head, Prescott pressed a light kiss to Nkosi's lips. "Anything for you."

Reaching their door, Prescott opened it and led the way inside. Once locked in their suite, he headed to the bedroom. After walking over the threshold, Nkosi paused, causing Prescott to turn back toward him.

"Anything, my mate?"

Prescott recalled their last words a few minutes before and smiled. "Anything."

Nkosi's smile could only be called predatory, even if he couldn't truly see him. "Undress me."

After swallowing hard, Prescott stepped forward and obeyed. He tugged the hem of Nkosi's shirt out of his jeans and pulled it over his head. Prescott made quick work of his mate's belt buckle, fly, and pushed them down his legs.

When Prescott felt Nkosi's hand on his shoulder, he knew what his mate was waiting on. He knelt and helped his lover take off one shoe and sock followed by the other. Finally, Prescott removed his jeans.

Prescott found his gaze snagged by Nkosi's long, slender black dick. His nostrils flared as he took in the maybe nine-inch length. Clenching his chute, he recalled how that piece of meat had felt inside him.

Gods, he's longer than normal, and this time I'll feel him driving deep into me bare.

Wanting a taste, Prescott leaned forward. The hand on his shoulder tightened, making him glance up.

Nkosi smiled down at him. "Just a little suckle on my crown for now, baby." His smirk turned heated. "I'll let you have more another day."

Prescott groaned, loving his mate's dominance and control. Opening his mouth, he did as he'd been ordered and wrapped his lips around Nkosi's crown. He suckled lightly while licking at his flared head. The slightly salty essence of his lover's pre-cum slid across his tongue, drawing another moan from him.

"Mmmm, I can tell you enjoy that," Nkosi rumbled, resting his other hand in Prescott's hair. "One more suck for now, baby. You can keep my dick in your mouth all night long after clean-up if you want, but I need in your ass now."

A shudder worked through Prescott as he thought about having his face buried in Nkosi's fragrant groin, his meat heavy on his tongue, all night long. Soft or hard, Prescott knew he would love the feel of that. He sucked hard on reflex.

Yes, please.

"Like that idea, don't you," Nkosi crooned, teasing his fingertips around Prescott's lips where they were wrapped around him. "Yes, you do."

Then Nkosi tugged on Prescott's hair. "Up, mate."

Prescott rose to his feet and waited.

Nkosi rubbed his palms down Prescott's chest, then slid his palms under his polo shirt. "Lift your arms and bend a bit at the waist."

As soon as Prescott obeyed, Nkosi hummed and pulled his shirt off of him. He skimmed his hands down his chest, mapping his pectorals, his ribs, and his abdominals. When Nkosi dipped his fingertips into his skinny jeans, Prescott sucked in his gut and whined.

"Gods, the sounds you make," Nkosi purred. "Music." Then he popped the buttons on his fly and gripped his erection. "I bet this is a thing of beauty." For a second, Nkosi's expression turned sad. "I wish I'd taken a moment to look last time."

Prescott couldn't resist his need to touch . . . or to soothe. Palming Nkosi's head, he began at the top. He massaged lightly as he worked down his neck to his shoulders and over his chest.

Even as Prescott relished the differences between his tanned flesh and Nkosi's nearly black skin, he murmured, "Not all looking is done with your eyes."

Nkosi sucked in a harsh breath, then jerked a nod. "You're right, my mate."

To Prescott's displeasure, Nkosi released him. "Take off the rest of your clothes, grab the lube, then climb on the bed." With surprising ease, he sauntered around Prescott and headed toward the bed.

Prescott's gaze fell to Nkosi's ass, and a groan ripped from him. The slender man's globes tempted his palms, and he wished he could grip and squeeze them. His fingers even twitched.

Nkosi chuckled. "See something you like?" As he asked, he rested one knee on the bed, pausing in his climb up.

Moaning, Prescott yanked his gaze away. "Gods, you have a gorgeous ass."

"I'll let you tap it before too long," Nkosi promised. Then his voice sobered as he admitted, "I'm not much of a switch, but I would never expect you to bottom all the time."

Prescott shoved out of his boots, socks, and jeans before heading toward the nightstand. "I'd love to top you when you're ready," he told his mate, wanting to be just as honest.

"But I really do love to bottom. With the way you worked me last time." Gripping his bobbing dick, Prescott groaned. "Fuck, so not a hardship."

Nkosi chuckled huskily. "I can smell your pre-cum, Prescott," he claimed, patting the bed. "Give me the lube, then lie down on your back."

Whimpering, Prescott obeyed. As he climbed up, he muttered, "I'm so hard, it's not going to take long."

"Good," Nkosi responded, a rumble in his voice. "Because I need in your ass in the worst way. So fucking hard just from your smell."

Prescott moaned as he shifted restlessly on the comforter.

"Gods, the sounds you make." Nkosi gripped his thigh, obviously getting his bearings. "Want to hear more and more."

As soon as Nkosi positioned himself between Prescott's spread legs, he skimmed his hand up his thigh and gripped his erection.

Groaning, Prescott bucked.

Nkosi chuckled.

Before Prescott could decide what he thought of that, Nkosi swallowed him to the root.

Prescott roared as he jacked his hips up. Nkosi took him. When his hips dropped back down, his mate's finger was waiting, and he shoved it deep inside him. Prescott pushed out, welcoming the intrusion.

His mate pegged his prostate.

Losing control of his hips, Prescott dug his fingers into the comforter. He popped his hips up, and Nkosi accepted it. Upon lowering him, his mate stretched him. One finger became two, and two became three.

Nkosi massaged his prostate on every few thrusts as he skimmed the palm of his other hand all over his torso. He plucked and teased his nipples. His fingers dug into the sensitive grooves of his vee. Even his balls were rolled and played with.

Just as Prescott had warned, his testicles pulled tight embarrassingly fast. His body shook, and his cock throbbed. Even as he opened his mouth to warn his lover, his orgasm crested, and he came, pouring spurt after spurt of cream into his mate's mouth.

As soon as Prescott stopped pulsing, Nkosi allowed his still-hard dick to slip from his mouth. He eased his fingers from Prescott's channel, then gripped his hips in both hands. When Nkosi easily flipped him, Prescott gasped, and a fresh wave of arousal surged through him.

"Oh, gods, you smell so good," Nkosi crooned between licks up his neck. "Need you now."

"Yes." Prescott managed to get his knees under him, and he spread his legs as wide as possible. "Now."

Nkosi didn't wait for a second invitation. For a split second, Prescott felt his mate's cock head touch his stretched and lubed opening. Then his lover was sinking into him in one long, smooth glide.

When Nkosi's crown slid across his already over-sensitized prostate, Prescott whined and bucked. His still-hard cock twitched. He dug his fingers into the comforter and canted his hips even further.

"So good," Prescott cried. "Love your dick in my ass. Yesss, fuck me."

"No need to beg, my mate," Nkosi purred into his ear, then he did exactly that.

Nkosi speared into Prescott over and over. His angle was perfect, constantly stimulating his gland.

Prescott felt Nkosi's flesh slap his ass with each rut. His mate's fingers dug into his hips, holding him still for their pleasure, and he knew he'd have bruises. Even the huffing grunts escaping his lover enflamed his blood.

"Come for me," Nkosi demanded. "Do it now."

To Prescott's shock, even though he hadn't thought he'd been close enough, his body seemed wired to obey. He came, groaning and grunting, growling his pleasure. His chute muscles clamped onto the erection still sliding in and out of his channel, stimulating beyond the point of any coherent thought.

The teeth at Prescott's neck were the last straw. The flash of pain yanked a gasp from him, but the resulting heatwave . . . exquisite.

His body shaking, his eyes rolling to the back of his head, Prescott came again before darkness took him.

CHAPTER TWELVE

Nkosi came to slowly, his body blissfully lethargic and re-laxed. The feel of a warm frame pressed against his back as well as a strong arm around his waist brought it all back. Even still semi-asleep, he smiled.

The sun beating at the backs of Nkosi's eyelids made him wonder what time it was. He carefully cracked his lids, uncertain where the light was coming from. After he'd blinked a few times, the room came into view.

The dresser against the wall in front of him was a six-drawer tall-boy. The nightstand stood beside the bed a couple of feet from him. There was a clock on it, which read five-forty-two.

Suddenly realizing the significance of reading, Nkosi gaped. He swept his gaze around the room, tipping and turning his head to see more. Several open doors led out of the bedroom, and he spotted a sink denoting a bathroom and a chair indicating the front room. The other door stood wide open, revealing plenty of clothes.

Nkosi smiled.

Damn. My mate is quite the clothes horse. So cute.

And fucking hell, I can see.

Relief slammed into him hard and fast. Even knowing his mate accepted him no matter what, he was glad he wouldn't have to live his life blind. While he had the utmost respect for the humans who pulled it off, he didn't know how he would have managed it.

Nkosi knew he was just too damn independent and solitary.

Okay. Maybe part of it was fear, too. Fear that my mate would grow tired of me. Grow to resent me. Grow to hate my grumpy annoying ass.

Gods, now I'm not being fair to my love even in my head.

My mate went into battle for me. Think of him as a goddamned equal.

Nkosi knew it would take time to get there, but he fixed that as a goal in his mind. Sure, Prescott seemed like a flamboyant pretty boy, but he'd already proven he had a core of steel. Not to mention, to escape a locked-down estate, he had to have a brilliantly observant mind.

My mate really is badass . . . and sexy as fuck.

With those thoughts firmly in mind, Nkosi glanced around the room again.

So, how did my eyesight heal overnight?

Feeling Prescott's arm tighten a smidge around his waist as well as the soft snuffling of irregular breathing on the hairs of his neck, Nkosi knew his mate was waking. He wanted to see his mate's beautiful blue eyes again . . . so very much. To that end, Nkosi carefully rolled and twisted until he lay on his stomach, his face on the pillow and turned in Prescott's direction.

Nkosi smiled.

Prescott's eyelids were twitching against the early-evening light coming through the bedroom window. The long strands of his light-brown hair fell across his forehead. It was the smudged eyeliner that really caught his attention, and he was tempted to lick a thumb and ease one of the smudges away.

Huh. Never dated a man who wore eyeliner. Of course, I've never actually dated at all.

Letting out a soft sigh between slightly parted lips, Prescott hummed. "I can feel you staring at me," he mumbled, his voice scratchy from sleep.

Nkosi chuckled softly at the innocuous comment. "Yes," he agreed quietly. "I'm staring at you while you sleep." Upon seeing the corners of Prescott's lips twitch, Nkosi whispered, "You're beautiful, my mate. I feel so damn fortunate Fate gave you to me, and not just because you accept me no matter what."

"Of course, I do," Prescott mumbled as he blinked his eyelids open. "You're my—Oh!"

Grinning, Nkosi winked. "Yeah."

"That's fantastic." Returning his grin, Prescott lunged forward and tackled Nkosi, climbing up his body. "I know you really wanted your sight back, and I'm so pleased it happened for you." Bracketing Nkosi's head, Prescott peered down at him, his blue eyes gleaming with happiness. "I love seeing you happy."

"I know." Nkosi wrapped his arms around Prescott, rubbing up and down his back, enjoying the feel of the man in his arms. "I'm so sorry you ended up so stressed out from this."

Prescott shrugged. "You were injured. We got past it." Then his expression turned contemplative. "How's your head? You still have a bit of a lump."

Nkosi knew what Prescott was really asking. He'd asked it himself. Why had he healed overnight? Nkosi opened his mouth to admit he wasn't certain. Then his focus fell on his claiming bite.

"I ingested your blood," Nkosi mused, thinking quickly.

Nodding with a smirk twisting his lips, Prescott winked. "I hear that's pretty common when shifters mate." Then he waggled his brows. "Just be warned. The second we screw face to face, or I take you, whichever comes first, I'll be laying a claiming bite on your neck, too."

Nkosi felt his blood heat just at the idea, and his prick began to fill.

Prescott must have felt it, for he chuckled seductively.

Groaning, Nkosi shook his head. "Gods, you are a sexy fucker, baby," he murmured, rubbing his back. "But I think I should answer your question first."

Heaving a put-upon sigh, even while winking, Prescott grinned. "What were we talking about?"

Chuckling at Prescott's playfulness—*I can't wait to have so much more enjoyment in my life*—Nkosi gave his lover a serious look. "What I'm saying is the blood of a mate boosts the healing abilities of the other. I bit you." He rubbed his fingertip over the scar he'd left in Prescott's flesh. "I drank the blood of my mate."

Nkosi enjoyed the shudder that worked through Prescott's body as he teased over his mating mark.

"Oh, Nkosi," Prescott muttered. "So glad my blood healed you."

"I'm more pleased you care for me as is, baby," Nkosi admitted, sliding his palm around to cup Prescott's nape. "Come 'ere."

"Yes," Prescott whispered, leaning forward.

Before their lips could touch, a trill pinging came from somewhere in the room. Prescott groaned as he jerked his head up. He glanced around wildly.

Nkosi swept his gaze over the room and spotted a panel with a light flashing on it. "Is that it?" he asked, pointing.

Prescott nodded even as his face paled. "Oh, shit." Meeting his gaze, he whispered, "That's the alarm for a perimeter breach."

"Damn it," Nkosi grumbled under his breath. "Where's your sweats?"

I thought we had everyone. Who would be attacking?

Everyone but Mindy.

A conversation Nkosi had sat in on came rushing back.

She had planned to force some of her pride-members to fight.

They weren't on my list, because I didn't know about them.

"We gotta get to your control room," Nkosi stated, jumping to his feet. "Thanks."

Nkosi took the sweats Prescott handed to him and jerked them on. They were a little big, but he yanked the drawstring tight to keep them around his hips. He skipped anything else and rushed from the room, Prescott on his heels.

Pausing in the hallway, Nkosi glanced both ways.

"This way."

Falling into step behind his jogging mate, Nkosi kept up. They reached the front hall with its sweeping double staircase, and Prescott led across it to the opposite wing. The crash of a body slamming into glass caught Nkosi's attention, and he hesitated.

"Damn it," Nkosi cried, spotting the big body of a tiger throwing itself at a side window a second time. The tall, slender pane appeared to have a metal design through it, but that wouldn't hold long against a shifter's strength. "Come on."

Nkosi switched directions and started them upstairs.

"But the control room is just down the hall," Prescott called, clearly confused.

"We'll have to take care of this first, and I'm not leaving you alone."

Been there, done that.

Pointing to the top railing, Nkosi ordered, "Stand up there. If things go south, shift and fly to that chandelier." He indicated the massive crystal monstrosity hanging over the two-story foyer.

"B-But—"

Gripping Prescott's jaw, Nkosi urged his mate to meet his eyes. "Baby, I need you safe, and that is as safe as you can get from a cat. Okay?"

"What about you?"

"Others will be here soon. This is a house full of lions with a few other things thrown in. It'll be okay."

Gods, where is everyone?

Nkosi held Prescott's gaze, not letting any of his own insecurity and concern into his expression or his scent.

"Okay." Then Prescott's expression hardened. "But only as a last resort." He tapped Nkosi's chest. "And no hero shit. We're a team now. Remember?"

Shit. Nkosi nodded. "No hero shit." *A team. That'll be a new experience.*

Then Nkosi accepted a hard kiss from Prescott, feeling the desperation in his lover's lips.

We'll be okay.

The window cracked, filling the room with the distinctive sound of breaking glass.

Pulling from Prescott's hold, Nkosi jumped onto the railing as he surveyed the struggling cat. The animal shook his head while scrabbling his feet. Taking advantage, he leaped head-first off the railing, ignoring Prescott's cry.

Nkosi shifted in midair, his change happening in mere seconds. His body ended up being tangled in his borrowed sweats. The heavy fabric bunched around Nkosi's slender body gave extra padding when he landed on top of the intruder.

Immediately, Nkosi twisted his head and sank his fangs into the flesh beneath him, piercing easily through fabric and fur. He didn't know who the tiger was, so he kept his venom controlled. After pumping just enough into the beast to knock it out for a few hours, he retracted and coiled.

His body, still trapped in the sweats, hit the floor. He peered around, searching for an opening. The hesitation cost him.

"Well, well, well." A cold female voice that Nkosi recognized filled their air. "So you are here."

Mindy.

Nkosi felt himself being picked up, Mindy using the sweats like a sack. Playing dead, or stunned, he remained still within the folds. It didn't help.

Mindy threw the bundle, and Nkosi found himself flying through the air. He did the best he could to relax his body, waiting for an impact. To his shock, it didn't come.

The honk of a duck sounded shrilly through the room right before the sweats were caught, and he once again began moving through the air. After a few seconds of soaring, he felt some jostling—his mate must have been doing his best to land on the chandelier.

Note to self—duck feet and chandelier tiers are not a good mix.

Still, they settled with only a minimal of swing, telling Nkosi that Prescott had managed it. Seeing light to his left, he slithered that way. He peeked out, taking in the lay of the land . . . and grimaced.

A group of Vincentius's men and women—Seever in the lead—stood facing off against Mindy and her tigers. They appeared evenly matched, some in human form and others in animal. Many of those in human form had guns.

Gods, this could turn into a bloodbath.

Then Nkosi registered Mindy's demands. "You give me the traitor, and I'll walk out of here. You'll never hear from me again." She growled low in her throat. "I just want the one who caused my mate's death. Restitution."

"If you hadn't been rogue, that would be perfectly suitable," Seever stated, his voice cold and hard. "But since you *were* rogue, still *are* rogue, you will find nothing here but death for you and anyone following you." Then Seever swept his gaze over the group following Mindy. "Do you hear that? You follow a rogue? Is that what you wish to be deemed, too?"

There were a few who exchanged glances, and a big man admitted, "Her trackers are holding our families. We serve her, or they die."

Goddamnit.

Making a decision, Nkosi slithered out, making his way carefully away from the sweats. Once he balanced fully on the chandelier, he began to shift. He purposefully slowed it down, so his honking, flapping mate had the chance to keep his balance.

Nkosi could just imagine what Prescott would be screaming at him if he were in human form. He was sure he'd get an ass-pounding later, but he didn't mind.

Anything to keep my mate safe.

"Mindy," Nkosi called, drawing her attention. "I accept. Me for them."

Mindy grinned as she looked up at him. "Of course."

Nkosi knew it would never happen, especially when she started pulling her gun. Flipping off the chandelier, he rotated once in the air before landing on his feet. The impact on the marble floor caused pain to shoot through his skull.

Spots streaked across his vision.

Damn head wound.

Laughing, Mindy cried, "As if your death would be enough. I'm going to take everything that ever meant anything to you."

Instead of pointing at him, Mindy pointed up.

Prescott!

Acting on instinct, Nkosi leaped at her. She lifted an arm, thinking to bat him away, being the much larger of the two. That was okay. It didn't matter where he struck.

Still, Nkosi grabbed her wrist and shoved it down, using the momentum to make him land on her body. He wrapped himself around her, making her stumble backward and bark in annoyance. She pushed at his shoulder as she twisted her head to meet his gaze, her eyes full of hate.

Nkosi grinned as he let his fangs descend.

Mindy gasped.

Snapping his head forward, Nkosi sank his sharp, pointed teeth into Mindy's flesh just below her throat. Instead of sucking her blood, he poured his venom into her. Anger and fear for his mate pulsing through him, Nkosi didn't censor it. He gave her everything in his glands.

Before Nkosi had even finished, Mindy began to fall.

Nkosi felt the change in momentum and jerked his head up. He positioned his feet and caught himself in a crouch over her body. With a swift move, Nkosi grabbed her gun from her still-twitching hand.

Even as Nkosi leveled it at the big tiger shifter who'd flanked Mindy, he began to back up. To his shock, most of those in the tiger pride turned on the others. Within seconds, three were down, and the man who'd spoken peered at them with concern in his eyes.

"I know it wasn't a sanctioned challenge, and I'll accept the consequences. We all will," he said, appearing sad. "But they were going to kill our families, wives and cubs. We had a chance." He glanced at the others, who—regardless of if they were in human or tiger form—they nodded, appearing resolved. "To save our families, we'd do anything."

"You removed a rogue threat," Vincentius claimed, striding between his people to stop beside Seever. "I saw the entire episode in my security room." His smile appeared understanding. "We'll give you aid to help you remove whoever is holding your family under one condition."

"Anything," the man said, who seemed to be the spokesperson.

Vincentius pointed at Nkosi and Mindy. "The nature of Mindy's death will be that she was slain in battle with another shifter. *No* specifics."

The tiger shifter's eyes widened as he glanced between Nkosi and Mindy. Then he nodded quickly. "We will all individually swear it."

Feeling grateful, Nkosi cast a small smile the councilman's way.

Vincentius returned it with a nod of acknowledgment. Then he smirked, arched one brow, and swept his gaze over his nude body.

Nkosi rolled his eyes before handing the gun he'd picked up to Seever. After that, he peered up at Prescott. His duck's odd blue eyes peered down at him, appearing accusatory.

Giving his mate a beseeching look, Nkosi held out his arms. "I could use a shower, my love. Will you join me?"

To Nkosi's pleasure, Prescott spread his wings and flew to him. Catching him was a bit awkward, but he managed it. Tucking his mate under his arm, Nkosi headed out of the room.

"See you both for dinner," Seever called, amusement filling his voice.

Nkosi flipped him off, and laughter erupted behind him.

Once they were around the corner and in their hallway, Nkosi placed Prescott on the floor. He waited impatiently for him to finish his shift, which didn't really take all that long. As soon as Prescott returned to human form, Nkosi yanked him close.

"Thank you for giving me a home, a family. I haven't had that for a very long time."

With a wink, Prescott replied, "Anything for my mate." Then he dipped his head and whispered into Nkosi's ear, "And his ass."

Laughing, Nkosi grinned at him. "How about that shower first?"

"Or in the shower?"

Grinning at his mate's waggling brows, Nkosi winked. "You got it."

"In a sec."

Then Prescott grabbed Nkosi's face and slammed his mouth over his own.

As Nkosi accepted Prescott's tongue into his mouth, he reveled in his mate's taste and realized that this was exactly where he wanted to be.

In my mate's arms, pressed against him — home.

ABOUT THE AUTHOR

Charlie started writing fantasy when she was eight, and after stumbling onto her first erotic romance at age nineteen, she realized her true calling. She now focuses on writing gay erotic romance, normally of the paranormal variety, with heroes of all kinds. With the help and support of her husband, Charlie finally fulfilled one of her life-long goals . . . move to acreage with her horses. You can often find her curled up with her laptop and a cup of tea or glass of wine, creating her next adventure. Charlie enjoys exploring the mountains of her new Oregon home on horseback, 4-wheeler, or motorcycle.

She can be reached at ch.richards2010@yahoo.com
Or visit her at www.charlie-richards.com